The Way to Redemption

Matt Bircher

ISBN-13: 978-0-578-89420-1

Cover designed by Stephanie W. Dicken
Formatting by Polgarus Studio

*To the amazing educators who dedicate
their lives to the noble job of teaching others.*

Acknowledgments

The experience of writing my third novel was one that was very cathartic in the midst of both good and bad times. First and foremost, I thank God for the endless blessings in life that allow me to be creative and share my work with others. To my parents, Scott and Emma Bircher, your constant support and encouragement means the world to me and is what drives me to always work hard. My sister Maggie, thank you for always being yourself in every circumstance and for always pushing forward. To my grandparents, Joe and Linda Thomas, who I have spent much time with throughout the development of this book, you guys have always been there for me. You have shown your support in so many helpful ways and I thank you for that. To the book's first reader, Linda Thomas, "Meme", thank you for taking the time to share your wise insight. My grandparents, Jack and Julia Bircher, you guys always make the world a brighter place with deep love, faith, and positivity that is never failing. To Sharon Bland, thank you for the time you took to read and revise this book. It resulted in excellent notes that were very helpful. I am truly blessed with so many other family and friends in my life. If you're reading this, know that you are a big piece in supporting a young man's dream to tell stories that impact people in a positive way.

Introduction

At my first glance, their backs were all I could see. However, in a matter of seconds, my vision expanded to see a car with an open trunk backed in the driveway. I saw the bags in their hands and the ones already placed in the car. My wife and two kids, a boy and a girl, still were not aware of my presence as I stood at the wide open front door with my cell phone where it now always seemed to be ... in my right hand. After handing the bags to their mother, the kids took their smaller carry-ons, opened the back doors on each side of the car, and got in. They did so without skipping a beat and without looking back. What happened in only a few seconds felt like an eternity as I watched them. While I pretended to wonder what was going on, I was not oblivious to what was taking place right before my own eyes.

With the back of the car completely filled, I watched as my wife forced the trunk shut and took a deep breath after doing so. She made her way to the left side of the car; and, as she put her hand on the front door handle, she happened to glance back. When she turned her face in my direction, with her hand still gripping the car door handle, I saw a woman who I barely recognized. Not a single word was spoken as we looked at each other. The glare in her eyes told me everything I needed to know. I could tell by that look that our thoughts were the same ... as if we were complete strangers. Little did I know that she had thought this long before I ever did.

Two questions began to arise in my mind at that moment. One, how did I get myself to this point? Two, what was I going to do about it? I would get my answer to both questions much sooner than I expected. Just as in most other situations in my life, I had failed to acknowledge there was a problem, it was easier to just ignore the signs.

Chapter 1

The day before

Both hands were on the wheel as David Jackson drove home on a road he used every day. When he heard the first sound of his phone ringing, his right hand immediately reached for the cup holder where he had placed it. He took a quick look at the name that appeared on the screen and saw that it was not who he had been expecting. Still, David gladly answered it anyway.

"Caurice, what's going on buddy?" he said with the phone against his right ear.

"Coach Jack, you have a tool box, don't you?" Caurice asked.

"Yeah, I do. What do you need?" David replied.

"I need something to take this bed apart. There's no way it will fit through this doorway." Caurice answered.

Before responding, David glanced toward the passenger seat and was reminded of the reason he had been sent into town in the first place. In the seat, tied together, were several pink balloons that had different assortments of flowers on them. The last minute balloon request was from his daughter, Molly, whose seventh birthday party was soon to commence back at home. David was more than happy to escape the party preparation, and his daughter's "oh-so-much-needed" request was the perfect opportunity to do so.

Thinking there was still plenty of time before the party began, David replied to his newly former basketball player,

"I'll be over there in a second."

David made the detour and headed for Caurice's house. It was only five minutes out of the way and a place he had been several times when giving him post practice rides home. David turned onto the narrow road and drove toward one of the few driveways. When he pulled in and got out of his truck, he was met by Caurice and two other guys whom he knew very well.

These were not just three ordinary young men who happened to be coached by David Jackson. These were the stars of the Clear View High School basketball team. They had finished their senior year on top after leading the school to three straight state championships. Each was about to continue his basketball journey at the college level. The three of them, known around town as "the big three", had grown up together and shared a lot of similarities. One of the most important things they had in common was their love and respect for the man they knew as "Coach Jack."

"What are you fellas up to?" David asked as the boys approached him.

"Trying to get rid of some stuff before I head off to school." Caurice replied.

David lowered his tailgate and hopped onto the bed of the truck to open up his large toolbox. He grabbed a few things that he thought might help and, with them in hand, he followed the boys to the house. They made their way inside and into the room where a mattress stood against a wall and the bed frame was on the floor. David stooped down on the floor and asked them,

"Have any of you guys ever used a screwdriver or wrench?"

The three guys shook their heads.

"Well, do you guys know *anything* about a screwdriver or wrench?" David asked. Again, each of them simultaneously shook their heads. David could not let these young men go any longer without learning something he had the privilege of knowing how to do for most of his life.

"Well, today is your lucky day." David said as he made room for them to join closer.

After a short and simple demonstration, each of the young men took a crack at using the tools to

take the bed frame apart. During this time, David coached each one of them through the process

This was what he did best and loved the most.

Once the bed frame was finally taken apart, the boys followed David out of the house and back to his truck. They walked outside and passed a basketball goal and a basketball lying in the driveway away from the vehicles. As one of the boys picked up the basketball and walked over to an open space, he yelled to David.

"Hey, Coach!"

David turned around, as did the two others who were following along.

"How about a quick two-on-two game?" the boy asked.

"Ah, I wish, but I have to make it back for Molly's birthday party." David explained.

The boy smirked and teasingly said,

"Don't worry, Coach … we'll beat you quickly."

Hearing that sparked David's competitive drive for which he had been known most of his whole life. It was something that could bring out the best in him but also the worst. That drive allowed everything else around him to become a temporary blur as all he could think of was winning. David was not ludicrous for thinking he stood a chance with three soon-to-be college basketball players. He himself had played for Clear View High. Not only had he played … he had thrived. David Jackson was the star of the team back in his day; and, at barely six feet tall, he made the team and played at the college level. Now at over forty and still in very good shape, he had every right to be confident.

David looked down at his watch and said, "Okay, but just one game. We'll play to ten and count all made shots by one point."

He put up his tools, then jogged over to the goal and did a quick stretch. The four of them each paired up. Caurice joined the boy who issued the challenge as the other joined David.

After only a one-point loss in the game, David could not just simply go home on those terms, at least that is what his inner distaste for losing said to him. Therefore, one game turned into two, and two games turned into three, each of which David played with everything he had. It was a sight the boys always enjoyed seeing. At last David finished the third game with a win, allowing him to be content on finally heading home. When he looked down at his watch and saw the time, he knew he would be in trouble when he got there. His body dripping in sweat, David quickly got into his truck and left.

During the drive back, he knew there would be no good excuse as to why it took so long to find birthday balloons. Aside from his tardiness, he would also need to explain the reason for his sweat-stained shirt and red face. Excuses and explanations seemed to be all he could now offer his wife and family. Knowing this, the only solution he came up with was to show up and act as if everything was normal. Yet, there was no acting that needed to be done. This kind of thing *was* normal for him.

As soon as David turned onto his neighborhood street he could spot the cars parked alongside the curb in front of his house. With the driveway and his usual parking spot filled, he was left to park the farthest away, nearly two houses over from his own. With the balloons in one hand, he got out of his truck and took the long walk of shame while pretending to feel remorse. He walked into the garage and before entering the house, he could hear the sounds from inside. David put his ear up against the door and took a moment to listen as everyone began to sing "Happy Birthday." The sound of all the voices elevated as he opened the door and made his way inside. He slowly walked toward the kitchen where the song was already halfway finished. When the people that crowded his home's interior could be seen, David knew it was his time to take command over the entire event. He did not have to make a big scene to do such a thing. It was simply his presence that drew everyone to him. David snuck into the kitchen where everyone gathered around his daughter. As he strolled in and joined everyone, his wife noticed him before anyone else did. David finished singing "Happy Birthday" as if he had been there all along and saw her giving him a look with which he had become quite familiar. Her look screamed, *"Are you kidding me?!"* It was hidden behind an emotionless face.

Their daughter, Molly, sat at the table and beamed while taking in all of the attention. When the song ended, she blew out the seven lit candles in front of her and the room filled with applause. David made his way through the guests and to the table where his daughter sat. He handed her the balloons as he bent down and kissed her on the cheek. With this, the entire place was now aware of his arrival. He began to work the room as he shook hands and spoke to the guests who were a combination of family and friends. While doing so, he turned on his charm and put on the smile that seemed to always give him a free pass. He relied heavily on those two traits to get him off the hook. Those who encountered them always seemed to think they were genuine.

However, there was one person who had let him off the hook one too many times, and she was now paying a heavy price for doing so. David's wife, Beth Jackson, watched as her husband seemed to put everyone under his spell. She could not do anything but observe as everyone threw themselves at her husband. Beth saw the look on her daughter's face when her father approached her. However, there was something else that she witnessed that spoke volumes to her. It was an image that Beth would have a hard time getting out of her head.

Their son, Elijah, at the age of twelve, was not one who enjoyed crowds of people. In fact, he hated them. He avoided most people in general no matter who they were or their age. Elijah took in the party from afar, well behind everyone else. Hearing his father's voice alerted him that he was back and now in the room with everyone else. Beth saw her son trying to make his way toward the crowded area. She knew he was moving toward his father in hopes of having a moment with the man whose attention he quietly craved. However, it soon became clear to both Elijah and Beth that David, who had already become the man of the hour, did not care to fraternize with his son at that moment. With that realization, Elijah left the room and made his way upstairs where he would remain until the next morning.

Once the people began to drift out of the house, Beth and a few others began the job of tidying up. During this time, David continued to chatter until the very last guest left in hopes that he would not be expected to be a part of the clean-up crew. Neither his wife nor anyone who knew him would bother to ask such a thing from him anyway. David had done this routine many times before, enough for him to have it down to a science. His intentions and way of thinking was no secret to his wife. While she picked up cups and threw away plates, Beth began to wonder if she had finally reached her breaking point. That certain point had been continuously stretched further and further over the years, and so had her patience. Beth was a quiet woman under normal circumstances, but she had spent the entire party in almost complete silence as she pondered the matter.

When the last items were put away and the final guests made their exit, her thoughts remained. She went upstairs and helped Molly organize her birthday gifts and get settled down for the night. Before heading back downstairs, she approached Elijah's bedroom door. Gripping the handle of the door, she gently opened it and made her way into the dark room. The only light came from the small television. Elijah sat in front of it with a video game controller in his hands. As Beth walked toward him, he noticed her and, pausing the game, turned to face her.

"Hi, Mom." he said softly.

"Hey, sweetie. I just wanted to tell you goodnight." she said to him.

"Has everyone left?" he asked her.

Beth, still wrestling with her own thoughts, began to think deeper before responding.

"Um. Almost everyone." she replied, as in her thoughts she was imagining herself and the two children next in line to exit.

"Oh. Okay. Well, goodnight, Mom. Love you. Tell Dad I said hey." Elijah said.

"I-I will." she struggled to say. "Love you."

Beth walked out of Elijah's room and closed the door behind her. After doing so, she felt the tears well up in her eyes. She stood in the dimly lit hallway as she took a moment to get herself together. She wiped her face to get rid of any evidence of tears before going back downstairs. She had little to say to David for the rest of the evening, with the exception of a few short responses to his upbeat, nonsensical questions. She knew they were only asked in hopes of changing the subject and ending the tension between the two of them. There was too much angst built up in her heart and mind for that to be possible. His efforts were yet another of his actions that Beth saw right through.

After a short while she excused herself and went to their master bedroom. She was filled with many thoughts; but her body felt nothing more than pure exhaustion. The toll of it all was setting in. Her emotions were on overload due to her husband's late appearance at his daughter's birthday party, and the ever present concern of seemingly running their household alone. She quickly undressed and got into bed. With the lights off, she laid there struggling to stay awake as she waited for David to come into the bedroom. Before going to sleep, there was something that she needed to tell him. However, her husband, usually one to stay up late into the night, did so once again. In the midst of waiting, Beth's weary body gave in as her eyes became too heavy to keep them open.

In what felt like a quick nap, they unintentionally opened again at the sound of David in the bedroom. As usual, he made more noise than necessary. He had no reverence for his sleeping wife and was clearly in his own world. Beth turned on her side and looked at the nightstand clock to see that it was past midnight. She rolled back over flat on her back and stared up toward the darkened ceiling. After he had showered and completed his nightly routine to get ready for bed, David finally walked out of the bathroom. He plugged in his phone to charge and made his way onto the bed. As soon as he felt the soft mattress against his body, David took a deep breath and let out an exaggerated exhale as if he was also experiencing the exhaustion that Beth was feeling. Hearing him, she could not help but roll her eyes.

After a quiet minute or two, Beth spoke up … but only to relay a message that she had been waiting to pass on.

"Your son wanted me to tell you that he says hey" she said as her heart ached hearing those words.

David quietly replied, "That boy is always in his room. He should come down and say it himself every so often, don't you think?"

"Well, he was down earlier." Beth replied.

"Mmhh" David said as another deep breath followed.

"Maybe he's intimidated. He has to be approached by us. We can't just wait for him to do so, because it's not his nature." she insisted.

There was no immediate reply.

"You know?" Beth asked, hoping her words somehow resonated with David.

Again, there was no response.

She looked over to see that her husband already appeared to be in a deep sleep. Beth let out a sigh and rolled back over in hopes of getting some rest herself. However, it seemed that sleep was a thousand miles away as she was lying there, once again, lost in her thoughts. Beth realized that, aside from sleep, there was something else that was very much needed … change.

Chapter 2

David Jackson's watch vibrated repeatedly on his wrist at 6:00 a.m. until he was awakened. It did so every morning except on Sunday, which was the one day of the week that he could sleep in. David sat up and immediately checked his phone. After scrolling through useless news updates and notifications, he placed his feet on the floor and sat still for a moment. He let out a long silent yawn and stretched his arms. When he stood up, he did the same stretch to his back and could feel the effects of the previous day's basketball event. However, that feeling quickly slipped from his mind as his focus shifted to getting ready for the gym. No amount of soreness could keep him from that routine.

His Saturday morning trips to the local 24-hour gym were much different than others during the week. When the morning workout was completed Monday through Friday, he would head to work at Clear View High and make use of the convenient coach's office showers. On Saturday's, however, the post-workout possibilities were endless. David would go anywhere and think of any random thing to do, as long as it did not mean going directly home. If any breakfast pick-up requests were made by his family, they became an early lunch by the time he returned with them.

David once again followed his morning routine at the gym and, though lighter than usual, he still worked up quite a sweat. When he left, everything was as it always was. It was a normal Saturday as he drove around town making stops and starting conversations with whomever he encountered along the way. He finally arrived back home late morning, his usual time.

When he pulled into the driveway, he noticed his wife's car backed in the driveway with all the doors open.

The furthest his thoughts went about the car was simply ... *maybe that thing is finally getting cleaned out.*

Brushing that observation aside, he got out of his truck, went inside, and headed straight to the shower. David paid no mind to anything in his path on the way there. It was not until he had finished his shower and dried off, that he realized the house seemed mighty quiet for a Saturday. Still, he did not think much of it. He went back into the bathroom for a shave and then got dressed with the intentions of having a relaxing day. When he walked back into the bedroom and opened the door to the hallway, there was still no noise.

Usually at this time on a Saturday, the T.V. would be on and voices could be heard, even from where he stood in the bedroom. At that moment, there was nothing. The silence throughout the house was rare but seemed peaceful to David.

However, the silence soon caused him to become suspicious. He left the bedroom and walked through the kitchen, then into the living room. It was not until he looked directly at it, that he noticed the front door was wide open.

David furrowed his brow and walked closer to the doorway. There he could hear voices coming from outside in the driveway. When he reached the front entrance, David came to a sudden stop. Nothing could have prepared him for the scene he beheld, and it hit him like a ton of bricks.

Chapter 3

"Wh-Where are you going?" David asked as he stood there with a dumbfounded look on his face.

"I think the kids and I are going to spend some time at my parents' house." Beth replied without any hesitation whatsoever.

"Oh, uh … Well, how long?" he asked.

"David, I really don't know. But thanks a lot for taking the time to ask." Beth snapped as she quickly replied to him.

At the same time that Beth opened her door to get in the car, Elijah opened his from inside and got out. With headphones on his ears that played music, he had not heard the exchange between his mother and father. He was not even aware that his father was standing behind the car. With his head facing down, he took off his headphones and made his way toward David's direction. His mother, after starting the engine, noticed that her son was walking away. She got back out of the car and called his name.

"Elijah!"

He quickly turned around to face her.

"What are you doing?" she asked.

"I forgot my charger in my bedroom." he replied.

"Oh, okay. Hurry up and get it." Beth replied. She then glanced at Molly through the rear window and saw that she was already occupied with a game on her tablet.

As Elijah started walking toward the house, he looked ahead and noticed his father standing in front of him. He quickly paused and then stopped dead in his tracks while his eyes stared up at his dad. It quickly became obvious to David that it had been quite some time since the two of them had been this close together.

When he saw his son, he was met with the same look that Beth had given him just moments earlier. As David focused intently on Elijah, he saw features in his face that he had never even noticed before. His son suddenly looked like a young man instead of a boy. Without him even being aware of it, Elijah was growing up. The distance he had created between himself and his family was now clearer than it ever had been. As Elijah stood there, he did not know what to say or how to react. It only took a few moments for the rare presence of a man he did not truly know to make him uncomfortable.

Elijah began to take a few steps back.

Beth remained outside of the car and watched the awkward encounter with sadness. Though there was nothing new about what she saw, it served as a reminder of what had become a broken family. While her son continued moving slowly back toward the car, he turned around to look at her.

"I-I think I'll just find another charger." he said softly to his mother.

Elijah quickly opened the car door, sat down in the backseat, and let out a long exasperated breath. As Beth's eyes shifted back to David, she heard the sound of his ringing phone. David quickly looked at the screen and saw "Daniel Simmons." This was the call he had been expecting and waiting for. A look of disgust came across Beth's face when she saw David swipe his finger on the screen to answer the call. Shaking her head, she made her way back into the running car.

"Hey, Daniel, how are you?" David asked as he answered the call.

"Very good. I think you'll be pleased with this news." The man on the other line replied.

"Yeah?" David asked while he entered back into his own world.

"You've officially got an interview set up!" Daniel said with enthusiasm.

"That's great. Good to know." David replied, feeling a sense of relief that could not be heard in the tone of his voice.

"But there's one thing, you'd have to head up pretty soon." Daniel said.

"How soon?" David asked.

"Hmm, probably within the next thirty minutes." Daniel replied.

"Wow, well-"

"I know it's Saturday, but our athletic director is in the office working today and wants to go ahead and get it done. The sooner the better." Daniel said.

"Yeah, yeah- no … I totally understand." David replied.

"So can I count you in?" Daniel asked.

As soon as the man on the other line asked the question, David removed the phone from his ear. He watched as Beth's car began to pull ahead and out of the driveway. David had a decision to make. Would he go after his family or the job of his dreams? What he did not realize was that by answering his phone at that moment, the decision had already been made.

David continued to watch the car drive further down the street and into the distance until it could no longer be seen. During that time, he could hear Daniel's voice on the other line.

"You coming? he asked him, "David?"

Finally, David lifted his phone and placed it back to his ear.

"I'll be there." he simply replied.

Chapter 4

One month earlier …

On a late Thursday evening, David Jackson faced the athletic trophy case at Clear View High School. With his arms crossed, he paced back and forth in the quiet hallway. The school was nearly empty as only he, his assistant basketball coach, a few administrators, and the janitors were still present. The last practice of the season had just ended, and the players had all gone home. However, for David and his assistant coach, Marshal Lee, the work was just beginning. They expected to be on campus well into the night in preparation for the biggest game of the season, the state championship.

It was the same game that the team had won the previous two seasons under Coach Jackson's wing. With the majority of the team graduating and several off to play at the next level, the expectations were higher than they had ever been. Alone in the empty hallway, David could feel the pressure as he had, no matter where he was, all season long. Before planting himself in the coach's office to watch film and prepare for their opponent, David took a moment to reminisce and gain inspiration.

There was a big gap in the success of Clear View High's basketball program. Only two eras represented winning basketball at the school, and David Jackson was a part of both. First as a varsity player from 1987 to 1991 when the team won multiple trophies and awards during each season. Back-to-back state championships also came out of those years. David walked down to the left side of the trophy case and looked at each trophy that was

16

representative of his playing years. Many memories came flooding back during this reminiscent visit to his past accomplishments. Among all of the regular season and tournament championship trophies and even the larger state championships trophies, there was one that stood out the most. It was the one which read, *1991 Conference Champions*. It took his thoughts back to a very important moment in his life … one that went beyond a single trophy or game.

For the second year in a row, the 1990-1991 season was another great year for Clear View High basketball. Much of the credit was due to the great play by their star player, David Jackson, who was in his senior season. The team needed one final win to secure its second consecutive conference championship. The final regular season game was against their rival school, Western View High, who were tied with them for first place in the conference. The winner of this game would come out on top.

David remembered it clearly, how his adrenaline had rushed heavily in the amazing atmosphere at Clear View Gymnasium. The bleachers had been packed, with standing room only as a line of even more people still waited to get inside. When David's name was called in the team introductions, the entire gym erupted for their best player. In the midst of the chaos and excitement, his eyes had glanced over to the bleachers toward his high school sweetheart, who at that time was known as Beth Taylor. As the head cheerleader, Beth had watched every single game of David's high school career. Even when the cheer squad did not travel to away games, she managed to show up anyway by catching a ride with his parents. That among many other things in their relationship had led them both to believe that they belonged together.

David recalled how the exciting rivalry game remained close from start to finish. In the final seconds of the game, Clear View expanded their small lead to beat Western View. As the crowd cheered, they hoisted the conference championship trophy once again. The fans eventually cleared out of the gym as the team celebrated in the locker room. In the joyous atmosphere, David Jackson had been deemed a hero by those around him, but his mind was on something else. He was thinking about the future, not just the upcoming playoffs, but the rest of his life and with whom he wanted to spend it. His mind was on Beth Taylor. David's mother had given him a family ring earlier and he had it with him. In that rapturous moment, his impulse to give it to Beth was at an all-time high. He opened his gym bag to see the ring box tucked in an inside pocket right where he had stored it. He knew immediately what his next move would be.

Beth Taylor had waited for David in the hallway where she always did after games. Many of his teammates walked past her as they made their exit. She stood in front of the trophy case where the display lights caused shadows to reflect in the hallway were lights had been dimmed for the night. At last, David, the last player to leave the locker room, came around the corner.

"Where have you been? I've been waiting for so long." Beth said to him.

"I have been too." David replied as he neared her.

Beth had no idea what was on his mind. The only thing she was thinking of was a night of celebrating the victory with her friends. Instead, something very different and most unexpected happened.

Without saying a word, David reached for Beth's hand as he got down on one knee.

"What are you doing?" Beth asked with a laugh.

"Will you marry me and be my wife?" David asked.

She continued to playfully laugh, thinking there was no way that this was real.

"Oh, David. Get up!" Beth replied.

Then suddenly, David realized he was forgetting an important part of what he had planned to do. He reached down, unzipped his bag and pulled out the ring box. After opening it, David looked back up to see Beth, whose eyes had widened in shock, with her free hand placed over her mouth. The ring and the serious look on David's face told her that this was no joke.

"So?" he asked nervously.

In shock and hardly able to get the words out of her mouth, Beth nodded her head and replied,

"O-uh- well, of course!"

David felt a sense of relief as he placed the ring on her finger. When he had planned this moment in his mind, he had known that his question could have ended in disaster for him if she was not ready to answer it. As the two of them left the school that night, they had more than a championship game to celebrate.

Standing there, in the exact same place where his life had changed forever, David was lost in his thoughts as the 1991 Championship Trophy became a blur after staring at it for so long. His eyes then shifted to see his reflection in the mirror that was behind the trophies in the case. Feeling overwhelmed, he took a deep breath and continued walking toward the other end of the case. The more recent trophies and accomplishments from the second successful era of Clear View basketball were on display there. Most of those had come during David's time as head coach. At the end of the case, beside the two recent state championship trophies, was an empty spot. He could already envision the next one ... just one win away from it filling that space. With that in mind, David's focus changed from the past to the present. As he headed back to his office, his thoughts were on another championship trophy ... to fill that empty space.

Chapter 5

Beth Jackson sat in the middle of a packed auditorium at Clear View Middle School. The place was filled with family and friends of the middle schoolers who were performing in the annual spring play. The only seat left open was the one right next to her on which she had placed her purse. She repeatedly explained to the many who asked that she was holding it for someone. The production, in which her son was starring, was only minutes away from curtain time. Beth's phone was in her hand and against her ear, but the only thing she could hear amongst the many voices around her was the endless sound of ringing. She continuously redialed the number, even though there seemed to be no luck in reaching her husband. Every other second she would find herself turning around toward the back of the room, hoping to see him rushing through the doors to arrive just in time. Yet, she had a feeling that that would not happen.

Beth was not worried about her unresponsive husband. She knew exactly what was going on. This was not rare or out of the ordinary by any means. She knew of the big game that was on David's mind and that everything else around him was on pause. Watching his son do one of the few things that he loved to do had not only failed to make the top of David's list of priorities, it simply was added to the list of many family activities he had missed. It seemed to Beth that only things relating to basketball registered inside David's mind, even though it was a sport in which his son had never shown interest. In fact, Elijah had no interest in sports whatsoever; and that put a strain on his relationship with his father whose life revolved around athletics.

David never made much of an effort to understand and relate to his son in any way. He was unable to get past the fact that Elijah would not carry on, what in his mind was, his legacy. From Elijah's very first moments in the world, David could picture himself coaching his son. He could hear the sound of Elijah one day calling him "Coach" … a title in which he took more pride than being "Dad." Early on, in most pictures and at every opportunity, he had put a ball of some sort into his son's hands. Elijah had been signed up for every sport possible, in hopes that he would take the same path and have the same love as his father. However, as Elijah got older and managed to express his disinterest in athletics, it became clear to David that his master plan would never shape up the way he had hoped. When faced with that reality, David seemed to wane from the fatherly role.

Beth was very aware of her husband's feelings. She accepted how things were in their family, just as she accepted her son for who he was. Beth simply loved to see Elijah smile and desperately wanted him to be happy. It was only when he was on stage that Beth was able to see his full potential shine. She was not going to let her husband's absence ruin that experience, nor would she let it take away the joy it brought her. As the lights in the auditorium began to dim, Beth finally turned off her cellphone and placed it into her purse. She then removed the purse from the seat and sat it on the floor. As she was settling in, she looked over and noticed someone quickly taking advantage of the last available seat next to her.

"Is this being saved?" the man asked.

"I guess not." Beth regretfully replied.

The man squeezed in front of the people at the end of the row and took the seat.

"I'm Jason, nice to meet you." he whispered with his hand out.

"I'm Beth." she replied with a soft smile. "Nice to meet you as well."

The curtains then began to open up in front of them.

As the play was beginning at Clear View Middle School, David was right where Beth imagined he was and doing exactly what she knew he would be doing. He sat in the coach's office next to his assistant coach, Marshal Lee, as they watched footage of Ridgewood High School's basketball team. Coming up with a game plan for the championship game on Saturday morning was no easy task for the two of them. They had never before heard about or faced the school that was located on the other side of the state. David's phone was on silent, as it always was when prepping for a big game. He had placed it face down on his desk. Throughout the session, he paid no attention whatsoever to it. David's eyes were fully focused on the computer screen and his notepad. His only thoughts were studying how to become more familiar with his team's opponent.

Nearly two hours went by; and, after checking the time to see it was almost eight o'clock, Marshal was ready to call it a night.

"Man, David, I think we've covered our ground, don't you think?" he asked as he leaned back in his chair.

"You can head home if you want, I'll probably watch a little more. There's a good chance that it'll be a long time before we get another shot at a championship." David replied.

"You really think so?" Marshal asked as he sat back up.

"Just look at all of our guys who are leaving and compare them to the ones that are coming in to take their places. I mean, the JV team didn't do anything to excite us, and the middle school team only won three games all season." David replied.

"The players may not be comparable, but when it's all said and done, each of them will have one thing in common." Marshal said.

"Yeah, yeah. They'll all have the pride of wearing a Clear View Vikings jersey. I get that." David sarcastically replied.

"Not *only* that. Each of them will always get to say that they played for a heck of a good coach." Marshal responded.

Looking up at Marshal with a smile, David replied,

"I appreciate that but-"

"And they'll have played for you, also." Marshal said, laughing after cutting David off.

"Oh, yeah. I see what you did there, '*Coach*' Lee." said David.

The two men shared a laugh together and the mood in the room lightened.

"Well, since it's the last game, I guess I have a little more left in me." Marshal said.

David looked up from the computer, turned to Marshal and said,

"But, I think we've earned time for a little break."

"Fine by me." Marshal said as he stood up from his seat. "I'm gonna grab a snack, do you want anything?" he asked.

"No, I'm fine. Thanks though." David replied.

As Marshal walked out of the room, David grabbed his phone, turned it over and looked on the screen to see the notifications that filled it. They read, *Beth: Missed Call (4)* and *Text Message: Beth- "Where are you? The play is about to start!"*

Play? David thought to himself.

After a momentary pause, his eyes suddenly widened when he remembered the production in which his son was to play the lead role. Even though Beth had mentioned it to him on multiple occasions, it went in one ear and out the other each time. With the thought of basketball brushed aside, he quickly stood up. His mind began to race as it entered back to its normal hectic state. David closed the laptop, grabbed his notepad, and placed his work bag over his right shoulder. With his hands full, he made his way out of the office and into the hallway. He looked to his right and saw Marshal's back at the other end of the long hallway as he walked toward the break room.

"Hey, Marshal!" he said loudly to get his attention.

Marshal turned around to see the look of panic on David's face.

"Let's call it quits for tonight, I'll see you tomorrow!" David said with his voice still raised.

"You sure?" Marshal asked.

"Yeah. You were right, we've covered our ground." David replied while he backed up and headed in the other direction.

"Alright, whatever you say. I'll see you tomorrow." Marshal replied while he began to wonder what had caused David's abrupt dismissal.

"Now I've got to cover my own." David quietly said to himself as he turned around and rushed to the exit door.

David rushed out of the building and jogged to his truck, one of only a few vehicles left in the parking lot. He freed his right hand to punch in the four-digit code to unlock his door. Flinging his bag onto the passenger side, he stepped onto the running board to get in. The truck's interior was filled with heat after sitting in the sun all day, and David immediately reached for the air conditioner. He set his laptop aside on the middle console and reached into both of his pockets for the truck keys, only to find his phone in one of them. He then leaned over to scramble for the keys in his work bag. Yet, there was still no luck in finding them as the interior grew more uncomfortable. When he realized that the keys had been left in his office, David took a moment, sat back in his seat and then closed his eyes in frustration feeling like he would erupt.

"You've got to be kidding me!" he yelled while slamming his hand on the steering wheel.

David took a deep breath and opened the door. He got out to make the long walk all the way back to the coach's office to retrieve his keys. But when he got out of the truck, he looked ahead to see Marshal walking in his direction.

"Thought you might need these!" Marshal yelled as he held up David's keys.

"Yeah-yeah, I think so." David replied in relief.

As he tossed the keys to David, Marshal could not help but notice the defeated look on the face of his colleague and friend.

"Everything okay?" Marshal asked.

"Oh, yeah. All good." David said as he tried to sound assuring. "I appreciate it!" he continued as he got back into his truck.

David started his engine, and the truck jerked back out of his parking space as he put it in reverse. He waved to Marshal who slowly walked over to his car, not fully convinced that David was really okay. Marshal waved back and watched David speed out of the parking lot while hearing the sound of his engine revving loudly. When he reached the end of High School Road, David had proof of his disorientation when he nearly made the wrong turn. He stopped for a moment to remember where he was going and his purpose for being in such a hurry. Luckily for him, Clear View Middle School was only a couple of minutes away. However, when he turned down Middle School Road and saw the school grounds resembling a ghost town, he realized that the short distance did not matter and could not help his predicament.

David drove around the campus only to see one other car. He put his truck in park and reached for his phone to read the message he had received from Beth once again. This time around he was able to notice that it had been sent over two hours earlier. David tossed the phone aside and again leaned back in his seat with his eyes closed. He felt as if he had reached his lowest point. After a few seconds, his eyes opened; and David saw a man who was exiting the building. Seeing the man approaching him, David rolled down his window.

"How's it going?" David asked the man.

"Fine, the school is closed. I just locked up." the man replied.

"Yeah, I see that." David said as he looked around the near empty parking lot.

"Say, you're Coach David Jackson, right?" the man asked.

"That's me." David replied.

"Yeah, that was your boy up there singing on that stage tonight. I know you're proud." the man said. David was silent for a moment as he stared off into space.

"Yeah. Yes, I am." he finally responded,

"Did you leave something in the auditorium? the man asked. If so, I can run in and get it."

"No, no I don't think I left anything. I'm just heading back home now." David replied as if he had actually been in the auditorium.

"Alright, well good luck with the big game on Saturday. We're all counting on you to coach 'em up good." the man said as he walked away.

"Thanks, sir." David said with a nod while he rolled his window back up.

As David shifted his truck out of park and drove away, he realized he had dropped the ball. As he became aware of that, David began to think of how that affected him, not his son. His shame, filled with frustration, did not come from disappointment caused by missing Elijah's play. It simply came from the fact that he had messed up. He realized what an empty seat next to his wife had made him look like. Therefore, his sudden rush to get there did not come from a desire to see his son … it was all for the sake of his own self-image.

During the drive home, David began to think about what the man had just mentioned to him … that many people were counting on him to lead. It became his newest source for pity. He viewed it as a newfound fact, but he had long been conscious of it. David knew that it was all he could rely on. He had been backed into a corner due to his own selfish agenda, something he refused to admit to himself. As always, he had managed to tie his job and personal obligations together, which led to no clear separation between the two. His most important personal obligation *was* his job. It managed to bail him out of every situation he got himself into. The following morning, it did exactly that … once again.

Clear View High served as David's safe haven. He was the big man on campus as a coach, just as he was when he was a student. Whenever he walked through the school's front entrance, he was able to let go of anything and everything that troubled him in life and leave it behind. On game days, the energy throughout the school was high, with students hardly able to focus on their classes. Championship send-off day multiplied that times one hundred. The entire day served as a massive celebratory event. That energy was felt as soon as David got to work, and he needed the lift more than ever. He was worn down and exhausted in every imaginable way. However, that all changed when David was greeted with applause from the office staff as soon as he walked in the building. With a bright smile, he pretended to find the early morning applause embarrassing, but he fed off of it and desperately needed it. Luckily for him, there would be much more where that came from. Throughout the entire day, the attention and special shout outs never ended. It was very similar to a regular day for David. Whenever he strolled the halls or walked through a student-filled lunch room, everyone made an effort to speak to Coach Jackson.

The day ended with a massive pep rally for the basketball team. Both sides of the bleachers were filled with students whose screams echoed through the gym. The fight song being played by the school band served merely as background music compared to the cheering. After the cheerleaders took the floor, the school's principal, James Wallace, walked to the half-court logo with a microphone in hand. The team, all wearing matching sweat suits, looked on from a nearby hallway as they lined up in alphabetical order waiting for their names to be called. David stood at the back of the line and took in the electric atmosphere. Marshal, a decade removed from high school, could have easily been mistaken for one of the players. He blended in well as he jumped up and down with them. David, usually right there in the middle of it all, simply stood still and looked ahead. The line quickly lost its form and became a circle as Marshal began to dance in the middle of it.

"Come on, David. You're next." Marshal said to him.

The entire team turned and looked at their coach.

"I think we're about to go out there." David said as he pointed to the gym, "You guys line back up."

Listening to their coach, who represented a calm presence amidst the adrenaline filled chaos, the players settled down as did Marshal. However, as David stood there, he was nowhere near what he appeared to be on the outside. His thoughts had suddenly taken him to a chaotic place of his own. Adrenaline was replaced with apprehension toward both his job and personal life as he was finally beginning to separate one from the other. David had spent the entire day like every other day as he embraced the setting of the school and the people in it. However, something was different. It now seemed to him that those things which had kept him going were no longer doing the job. The exuberance of the entire school was right in front of him, yet he felt nothing from it. At the event-filled day's climax, David could no longer use his surroundings as fuel. It was as if he was away from it all and had gone to a totally different place.

Each of the players got his time to shine as his name was called through the loud speakers, but it all seemed like one big blur for David. After Marshal jogged onto the court, David was the last person remaining in the hall where he faced the opened gym door.

Principal Wallace paused for a moment and cleared his throat to say,

"And now, the one and only, a living legend, Coach, David! Jackson!!"

Though celebration caused the noise decibels in the gym to rise louder than they had been throughout the entire rally, David was so lost in his thoughts that it sounded more like a loud stormy roar. He walked slowly onto the court and instinctively waved at the cheering students, but was unable to accept their love and appreciation. For the first time in his life, he did not feel like he deserved any of it. For the first time in his life, he escaped the moment of glory as he looked ahead and wondered if it all was going to last.

Chapter 6

David stood with his team at half court as the chants of "three peat! three peat!" broke out in the crowd of students. Principal Wallace with the microphone in hand, walked over to David and handed it to him. During the same event in the past two years, the address to the students had been David's favorite part. Now as the microphone was handed over to him, the euphoria he usually experienced was absent. Usually being one to know all of the right things to say as he used his quick wit and strong appeal to capture the attention of his audience, David was now at a loss for words. With the microphone in his right hand, he stood there with all eyes on him. The crowd interpreted his silence as him being overcome with emotion from pure joy. They had no idea that he was overcome by an entirely different emotion. However, he played the part well. As he lowered his head, everyone rose to their feet and lifted their voices once again. David tried to gather his thoughts but to no avail. He was completely distracted by the memories that were overpowering what was happening in that moment. The scene from the night before flashed like a picture in his mind. All he could think of was the long over-due, difficult conversation he should have had with his family.

The night before, after missing Elijah's play, David had driven home from the empty middle school and tried to seem inconspicuous once he arrived. Without any explanation to Beth, he had placed his laptop on the coffee table, opened it up, and sat next to her on the couch with barely any conversation. By immersing himself in his work of film study and intense note taking, he had portrayed the image of busyness and stress ... and had avoided the much needed apology and conversation that his wife needed.

Beth had eventually left him on the couch and gone to the bedroom for the night. Once the bedroom door was closed, David closed the laptop and headed for the kitchen to heat up a late dinner. After finding some leftovers, he went to the microwave and placed the plastic container inside. Suddenly a rare feeling of guilt streamed through him causing him to stop what he was doing for a moment. He had left the kitchen and made his way upstairs where he found himself in front of his son's closed bedroom door. Knowing that Elijah would still be awake, he had planned to knock on the door, go in, and apologize; but he could not find the courage to do it amidst the shame he felt. He had stood there a few minutes before turning away and thus avoided another awkward explanation and encounter.

He thought about how he had walked over to Molly's bedroom door that was slightly ajar. She was sound asleep as he quietly tiptoed to her bed to bend down and kiss his daughter on the cheek. Before going back downstairs, David glanced again toward Elijah's door … and even took a step toward it before stopping himself. He then turned back around and headed downstairs to heat up his dinner that he ate alone at the kitchen bar.

"Um …" David mumbled into the microphone.

It was all he could say before being transported to another thought. This one took him one year into the future and to what he feared would be ahead. He imagined himself standing in the same spot on the gym floor where he was presently standing, but the bleachers were empty. The entire student body was in classrooms sitting at their desks. Each of them were staring at the clock on a Friday afternoon in early March just waiting for the bell to ring and the weekend to begin. There was no championship send-off pep rally. The basketball season had come to an end long ago, and the true colors of David Jackson as a coach had shown all year. He was the same man who had been beyond lucky to have next-level players on his teams every year as a head coach. They had not only carried the team to wins and championships, but they had also carried all of David's success with them when they left. Without them, he was nothing.

Suddenly David's mind was restored to the present. The people were in the bleachers waiting for him to speak. They had all grown quiet with anticipation as they waited. That silence did not stop him from hearing the "boos" in his head from the same crowd after another loss during the next season.

"Um ..." he said once again into the microphone. "We wouldn't be here if it wasn't for your support and spirit."

The students erupted once again. David paused for a moment as he waited for them to settle down.

He then continued, "So let's win another one ... thank you." That was it. He then handed the microphone back to principal Baxter.

The students jumped up and cheered yet again as the band played, making it impossible to hear the school bell that rang to end an eventful day. The students stayed in the bleachers as the basketball team filed out of the gym and headed for the charter bus that awaited them in the parking lot. The team boarded the large bus while David and Marshal made sure everyone's belongings had gone into the luggage compartment. Being the last two to enter the bus, they each took their seats in the open front rows on both sides of the aisle.

The driver looked back at David and asked, "Are we all set?"

"I believe so." David replied as he took out his headphones.

The bus slowly made its way out of the parking lot, and they were officially on their way to the season's final destination.

Throughout the first half of the two-hour trip, David kept to himself in the noisy bus where the guys carried the same energy that had been exhibited at the pep rally. David's actions were unlike the many other bus rides that he had taken to games. It did not matter if the trip's destination was just across town, he and Marshal usually spent the entire ride going over the game plans and talking basketball. Now, on the way to their third straight championship game, Marshal kept eyeing David who was seated just to his left across the aisle. It was obvious that he was restless. He noticed that David had spent the majority of his time with his eyes closed, seemingly trying to get comfortable. After just over an hour had gone by, the bus grew significantly quieter. Marshal turned toward the back of the bus to see that most of the team was now nodding or dozing. Looking back over in David's direction, he saw him staring out the window. Marshal stood up as if he needed to stretch and then sat down in the open seat next to David. David seemed to not even notice him until Marshal nudged his shoulder after sitting there for a few seconds. Turning to look at Marshal, he removed his headphones.

"What's up?" he asked Marshal.

"You've gotta tell me …. what is going on with you, man?" Marshal said softly.

David let out a deep sigh and replied, "You know, I've been thinking; and I never had thought about it before until I said it myself last night. I'm just thinking about how we will not be taking this same trip we're on right now next year … or for a long time … maybe never again."

Marshal responded, "Surely we'll be back at some point. I mean, maybe not next year; but we can't expect to be here every year. That's not normal. Even if it isn't the year after next, that's okay."

After a short pause, Marshal continued, "Great players and great teams come and go. They have to."

"But what if there's just not any great ones left out there? What if after tomorrow, that era is over for the program?" David asked.

"That's why we can't always rely on natural talent. We've sure been lucky to have a lot of it, and it's been great." Marshal replied. "What we can always count on is development; that's what our jobs are for."

"What if I can't do that? I never had to do it before. In the past eight years since I've been head coach, I've just been able to put the best five players in the game and let them loose." David said.

"Two things!" Marshal said, "One, you can't just include yourself in this equation. It's not all about you. Two, your mind shouldn't be thinking about anything past our game tomorrow. That's it. After that, *we'll* worry about what comes next for this program. It's not all on you."

David nodded his head in agreement to the advice he received from Marshal, who was twenty years his junior. Marshal stood up and gave David a pat on his shoulder. Before heading back to his seat, Marshal said to him,

"Just enjoy the moment while you're still in it."

For the remainder of the trip, David thought a lot about what Marshal had told him and the subject of his concern shifted away from coaching. When he thought about the most important moments he had failed to enjoy, they all had to do with his family.

When they finally arrived at the team's hotel, he got off the bus and left his troubles behind. David tried to return to his usual persona as the man who all his players knew and loved. The team dinner that night was filled with many laughs and plenty of jokes, many for which David was responsible. The high spirits continued as the team separated into their hotel rooms. Sharing a room with his assistant coach, Marshal, the two of them shared laughs of their own as they did last minute planning late into the night. They both knew the chances of winning were highly in their favor. It all served as a nice distraction and put a temporary pause to an even bigger problem that was unfolding in David's life. However, as soon as the lights were turned off, that diversion disappeared. David, lying in one of the two queen sized beds in the room with his eyes closed, could picture nothing else but Beth, Elijah, and Molly in his mind until he finally fell asleep.

The following morning David awoke to a complete change in mood. Beating his own alarm, he woke up at the crack of dawn with the realization that it was finally game day. Thoughts of his family and anything else other than the team had taken a back seat in his mind compared to the goal that he was only hours away from achieving. While Marshal continued to sleep, David took a short while to enjoy the few minutes of quiet time he would have in the day. While lying in bed, he could hardly control his rejuvenated spirit, now filled with excitement. He stared over at the hotel room curtains covering the large windows and imagined another championship banner waiting to be unveiled behind it. David then held out his right hand and could picture a new championship ring being placed on his finger. He checked his watch after pulling out his other arm from under the covers and paid no mind to the ring on his left hand finger … the one which he hardly noticed anymore.

David got out of bed to begin the hectic morning, which would ultimately lead to a noon game time start. His first step was to awaken Marshal.

"Coach Lee!" David said as he tugged on his shirt.

Marshal slowly opened his eyes.

"The day has come, my friend! The day has come!" David said with a smile.

David then enthusiastically proceeded to the next step which was to wake up a full team of teenaged young men. Out in the hallway, he knocked loudly on all of the doors that were occupied by the team to signal the players that they had thirty minutes before meeting for breakfast.

At the same exact time, just past seven o'clock, back at the place where David called home, Beth was on wake up duty as well. She did so in a gentler and less eager manner than her husband. Beth went to Elijah's room first and then to Molly's, saying the same thing to the both of them, "It's time to get up and get ready, Sweetie."

After she picked out some Clear View Vikings apparel for Molly to wear, Beth headed back to her room to get ready. Just before reaching the staircase, she heard Elijah's voice calling her back to his room.

"What is it?" she asked.

Elijah sat up in bed and asked, "Do I have to go? Can't you just drop me off at Grandma's house?"

Beth walked closer to him and replied, "Now, honey, we need to support your dad."

Elijah knew well of his father's shortcomings and thought back to his play just two nights earlier. Prior to it starting, his mother was the first person he saw when he peaked out at the crowd from behind the curtains. The empty seat beside her was quite obvious to him. After scanning the rest of the room, it was clear that his dad was nowhere to be found in the auditorium. Through the many lines and song lyrics he had memorized, that disappointing sight had been in the back of his mind during his entire performance.

Beth could see the look on Elijah's face while he sat there in his bed. She knew in her heart that they shared the same feelings but never spoke of them.

"So get on up. We'll need to be leaving soon." she said to him.

Beth stood at Elijah's bedside and took a deep breath as she reached for her son's hand. She forced a timid smile onto her face and then turned around to go back downstairs. As soon as she let go and faced the other direction, her facial expression matched her true feelings as she walked out of his room. Watching her leave, Elijah hardly bought into his mother's reassurance, but he figured that there was nothing else he could do except go to the game.

As Beth began to get ready, she looked at herself in the mirror as she applied her makeup. She could see almost the same expression on her face as she had seen on Elijah's when he tried to find an escape from the game. She didn't really want to go, but she felt it was her responsibility. After applying her make-up and blotting her lipstick, she took a quick look at the back of her hair with her hand mirror. She could only hope that the kids were up out of bed and getting dressed. She scanned her closet looking for a green shirt to resemble the school's colors, and after finding an outfit and quickly changing into it, Beth walked out of her room, putting on her earrings at the same time.

Thinking Elijah and Molly were upstairs, Beth yelled, "Are you guys almost ready?!"

To her pleasure, when she entered the living room, she paused to see the sweetest sight. There was Elijah helping his little sister put the large cheer bow into her hair. At the sight of that, she could not help but smile genuinely.

"Well, here you guys are!" Beth said, actually surprised to see that the kids were already downstairs, dressed, and ready to go.

Elijah and Molly both turned around and looked at their mother with faces that showed no enthusiasm whatsoever for the venture which they were about to take. Beth could easily see that neither of them had any interest in the destination for which they were soon heading. That brought a damper on the tender moment she had just experienced.

"Elijah, you and Molly get the bags I prepared with food for the road." Beth said, "I'll get the car ready."

Moments later, the kids came out with their hands full of the snack bags and got into the car. Beth walked back to the door to lock it and then joined them in the car.

"Alright here we go." Beth said quietly once both of the back car doors were shut and the seatbelts buckled. She backed out of the driveway and the two-hour trip was underway.

Throughout the long drive, the car was very quiet as both of the kids were occupied with the small screens in front of their eyes. Only the sounds from the radio softly playing, the hum of the motor, and the tires on the road were heard. While she was driving, Beth's mind was in high gear. She thought back two years earlier and remembered how different the exact same trip had been. That year, she and the kids had been filled with excitement on their way to David's first championship game as a head coach. Even the year after that had been a fun day. Those days proved a drastic contrast to the way things had turned out to be. To Beth, life resembled the mood that this trip had now brought to her and the children. It seemed as if everything in it had become stale.

Her musings were suddenly interrupted by the sound of Molly's voice blurting loudly out of nowhere.

"Mom!" she exclaimed, "I need to go to the bathroom!"

Hearing this, Beth realized that the last minute use of the bathroom was the one thing she had forgotten to cover before leaving home.

"That's fine, we'll find somewhere." she replied as she looked down at the clock.

Just past the halfway point, Beth took the next exit with a sign showing a lone gas station there. They parked just outside the entrance to the large food mart at the gas station; and when the three of them entered the building, there was a long line of people just outside the restroom doors. Most of the people standing there looked as if they were on their way to the same place. Many of them were wearing green shirts with the Clear View High logo.

As soon as Beth saw the line, she asked Molly, "Are you sure you can't wait until we get closer?"

"Yes, Mom. It's an emergency." Molly whispered. Sighing, Beth walked towards the end of the line.

"Can I go back to the car?" Elijah asked.

"Sure, go ahead." Beth replied as she handed him the keys. "Just be sure to lock the doors."

After a long time waiting, Beth and Molly finally made their way back to the car. They each pulled a car door handle to find that it was locked.

Thinking Elijah would notice that they were back, Beth tried to open it again; but the door still remained closed and locked. She took a look in Elijah's window to see his head against the seat and his eyes closed. He appeared to be fast asleep. Beth began to knock loudly on the window and finally saw him move. Elijah turned around as his eyes opened wide when he saw his mother outside not looking too happy. When he finally unlocked the car door, Beth and Molly quickly got in.

"Sorry about that." Elijah said.

"How much sleep did you get last night?" Beth asked.

"Eh, not much. I was just *too excited* about this game." he replied.

Beth looked at her son in the rear view mirror with an eye roll in response to his sarcastic comment. She then glanced down at the clock, and it became clear just how much of a set back their stop had been. She quickly backed out of her parking place and was soon back on the highway.

As they neared the arena, the city traffic began to pick up and Beth's patience was on edge. She was able to maneuver her way around and finally made it to the parking deck. As soon as she got the car parked, the car doors sprang open, and the three of them began their walk to the venue that was only a couple of blocks away. Upon entering the building, it became clear to Beth that there were many more spectators in attendance than the previous two years combined. Though the arena, which was the one where the state college played, was nowhere near full, she was still taken aback by the large turnout.

After having their tickets checked, Beth and the kids made their way to the section of seating behind the Clear View bench. It was like a sea of green with all the school color shirts on display. They had made it just in time for the team introductions. As she maneuvered down a row of seats with Elijah and Molly ahead of her, Beth smiled and waved to the many familiar faces that greeted them.

"And the Coach for the Clear View Vikings is David Jackson."

Just as Beth and the kids were sitting down, the Clear View crowd stood up from their seats and erupted into a roar when the PA announcer said her husband's name. When the introductions ended, Beth leaned back in her seat and felt like she could finally exhale after a hectic morning and long drive. The players took the court for tip-off; and as soon as the ball left the referee's hands at half court, Elijah tapped his mom's shoulder.

"Can I go walk around?" he asked her.

"No, you may not go alone! Just watch the game … it's why we're here." she replied.

Elijah waited a few seconds and then asked, "Well, can I at least go get a hotdog or something?"

"Go ahead." Beth said as she reached in her purse and handed him some money, saving herself from hearing him ask the same thing over and over again.

"Come right back." she told him as he got up from his seat and walked away.

"Will do." Elijah said as he put his headphones back on and walked up the stairs.

Beth shifted her focus back to what was in front of her. It was not necessarily the game that had her attention, it was David. She watched as he paced back and forth in front of the team's bench. While looking at him, Beth's mind took her back two nights earlier to the last time she had seen her husband.

It all came back to her. She had sat alone on the couch after the kids finished their late dinner and went upstairs to their rooms for the night. After having a long day at work and then going straight to Elijah's play, she was drained. Not even the classic comedy reruns that played on T.V. could bring any emotion out of her. The only thing she could do was stare at the long text message she had typed to send to David in which she had laid out her true feelings. In the message, she had included a laundry list of things that were long overdue for their discussion. All she had to do was press the "Send" key. As Beth read and re-read the message and moved her finger back and forth from the screen, she just had not been able to go through with it. She had thought to herself, *He really shouldn't find out this way. I will just tell him in person when he gets home … if he ever gets here.*

After back spacing the entire message, she had looked at her watch and then back up at the T.V. minutes later, she had heard the front door begin to unlock; but before it opened, Beth had looked back towards the T.V. and pretended to be unfazed by David's late arrival.

"Hey there." David had said as he headed straight to the living room, carrying his laptop in hand.

"Oh, hey." She remembered that she had quietly replied while watching him remove his bag and place the laptop on the coffee table.

David, still appearing to be in work mode, opened up the laptop and pulled out his notepad.

"Was your day good?" Beth asked.

"Oh, yeah. Just, uh, busy … real busy." he replied, still yet to make eye contact.

"Yeah, I can see that. That's good … that's great." Beth said in a monotone voice.

Several awkward minutes dragged by … she was consumed in thinking of what needed to be said while she continued to hold back from expressing her truth. She knew she finally had to hold him accountable; but when he walked in the house, she had once again lost the will and courage to do so. She had continued to sit there on the same couch as David waiting, hoping he would say something so she would not have to. After even more time passed, she was too tired for a confrontation, so she had decided to just give it up.

"Well, I'm going to go get ready for bed." she said in hopes that there was a chance of him taking some responsibility for his behavior. His response showed no sign of it.

"Okay, I'll be in there when I finish up." David replied without looking up from the laptop.

Much later David had made his way into the bedroom. Unable to get to sleep, Beth, lying still in the dark room had heard him walking in. Nothing had been said as her eyes remained closed resembling her internal vault that was full of missed opportunities.

It was all still fresh in her mind as she watched him, totally focused on the players and putting all his energy into the game he was coaching.

Chapter 7

It was a sobering moment for David when he looked up at the large scoreboard and the time remaining in the season changed from minutes to seconds. Seeing his team had a large seventeen-point lead, it finally dawned on him that his team was going to win. Not only would the game be won, the expectations for their special "three-peat" season would be met. As one of his players dribbled out the final seconds, David began to walk toward the opposing coach and met him halfway at the score table for a handshake. When the loud buzzer finally sounded through the arena, the Clear View bench stormed the court. While David, Marshal, and a few volunteer coaches shook hands with the Ridgewood team, the Viking players celebrated as if they had never been there before.

After David worked his way down the opposing team's bench, he stopped and looked out onto the court. He saw his team in a state of total jubilation. Marshal and the others who were associated with the team had joined in. David simply paused and stood by himself for a moment, as if he did not know what to do next. Then and there, he knew the feeling of triumph would be temporary. After taking in the fact that the special era was over, he slowly walked toward his team out in the middle of the court in an attempt to savor its final moments. However, for David, such a thing was impossible to do. Even as each of the players began to run in his direction for one big embrace, he felt as if none of it was really happening to him. The team was finally able to calm down for a moment when the trophy was brought out by the state's high school athletic commissioner.

David watched as the commissioner walked toward them with the large trophy in hand and asked Marshal, "Was the trophy that big last year?"

"I guess we need to expand our trophy case!" Marshal said with a laugh.

With his mind now focused on looking into the future and doubting it, David thought to himself, *I don't think that will be necessary.*

The commissioner stood next to David and was handed a microphone to address the crowd for the trophy presentation.

"It is my pleasure to award yet another state championship trophy to the Clear View High School Men's Basketball Team." he said.

Applause rang from the large number of Viking supporters who had traveled the long distance for the game.

The commissioner continued, "For the third year in a row, I want to congratulate the players and their great coach, David Jackson."

The crowd roared even louder as the commissioner handed the trophy over to David, who then took a long look at the trophy that he gripped with both hands. He looked up to the stands and saw that all eyes were on him once again. Among those watching was Beth and their two children. Before recognizing anybody else around them, David noticed his family first as they clapped their hands along with everyone. For the first time he could see through their smiles and while gazing into each of their eyes, David saw their looks of misery. He glanced back down at the trophy and immediately handed it to Marshal. David felt nothing for it and had lost his desire for the prize they had won. He knew very well that it was the cause of his family's pain.

While Marshal hoisted the trophy up in the air and the players around him cheered as each of them reached to touch it, the commissioner held out the microphone for David. At any other point in his life, David Jackson had jumped at any opportunity to be the center of attention. The reason behind his strong desire to win was to have more of those opportunities. Now there was an awkward feeling within him at a time that should have given him great fulfillment. Feeling undeserving of the recognition he had always craved, David shook his head indicating that he did not want to speak. When the crowd noticed his resistance, their cheers grew for their team's leader to say something. David finally gave in and took the microphone.

He cleared his voice and finally said, "This wouldn't be possible without these guys behind me. They're the reason for this trophy."

David truly meant what he said, and those who heard him took it as an act of humility. When he looked at his senior players, David knew his success was because of them. He felt like a complete fraud and couldn't help but think that those who admired him now would see him as one in due time.

That notion led to a solemn time in the weeks after the championship. It was rare for him to have a dead period in his schedule. Outside of teaching physical education, there were only two things planned before the end of the school year. The first was the college signing day for several of his players going to the next level. The second was a basketball workout for incoming high schoolers and varsity players, something that David began to dread as soon as it was scheduled. There was suddenly more time to dwell on his mistakes as a father and husband, but he still did not get up the courage to owning them.

Both his work and personal life felt as if they were on the verge of collapse, but nobody would have ever known it. The Clear View supporters lived in the moment and were on top of the world after another championship. David, however, had a different perspective than most and was one of the few who had an idea of what the future held for the basketball program. Those same supporters also saw the Jackson family and would never suspect they had issues, even if they knew them personally. They saw a popular, charming husband with a beautiful and hardworking wife, and two children who had resemblances of the both of them. In reality there was much more going on under the surface. Increased time together as a family proved to be detrimental. The family grew further apart the more time they spent together. They all seemed to become different versions of themselves. Pointless chatter at the dinner table took the place of the words that needed to be said and heard from each other. The path toward restoration was uncharted territory for them, and it seemed they were unable to find it.

When signing day came around for his former players, David had a legitimate reason for staying late after school ended. It was a bittersweet day for him. It was the true sign of a chapter coming to a close, but David still looked forward to the signing event. Even though he hated to see his best players leave, the sense of pride he felt for them was unmatched. The occasion also kept him from being at home where he grew more uncomfortable as the days went by. The school day ended at 2:30, and David mopped the gym floor as he did every day at that same time. Walking back and forth on the gym floor was a form of solitude in the quiet, empty gymnasium.

Before finishing on the court, David made it a point to look up at the many banners that hung from the rafters. The inspiring sight represented the many accomplishments from the team and the individual players. He then glanced up at the "*Clear View 1,000 Point Club*" above the gym door. He usually tried to avoid paying much attention to this because he thought it put too much attention on individual success. He felt strongly that teamwork should be the focus. An even bigger reason was due to the fact that he had been less than twenty career points short of getting his own name on it. He looked over the list of other memorable players and saw the four most recent names: Zeke Thomas, Josh Quinn, Caurice Clark, and Charlie Gray. They had just finished their high school careers on top, and each of them were signing to continue playing in college.

David could appreciate seeing those names. For that many players on the same team to reach that kind of milestone was a sign of success. There with the large mop in hand, he was already reminiscent of the good times that had flown by and ended. He let out a sigh and walked off the court. Checking his watch, he saw the three o'clock signing was only minutes away. He quickly placed the mop back into the closet in his office and headed down the hall to the library.

When he reached the clear glass doors, David noticed the large crowd of people already gathered for the event. There were balloons on both sides of the table that had been covered with a green Clear View Vikings tablecloth. Behind the table were four empty chairs for the signees. At the end of the table were two hats. Three of the players had made their decision about where they would continue their education and continue playing basketball. Charlie Gray, however, had not yet made up his mind. He had narrowed his list down to two schools whose logos were on the hats. Normally most players would go to their high school coach for advice on their big college decision. In doing so, players expect to receive a reasonable and unbiased approach from their coach. It was a different situation for Charlie.

The two schools on his list were Henderson University and David Jackson's alma mater, Eastern State University. Representatives of both schools were in attendance. Upon entering the library, David was able to spot someone he knew quite well from Eastern State. His former teammate at the school, Daniel Simmons, was standing in the back of the room wearing a purple collared shirt with a ESU logo. David began to make his way over to him and looked for other Eastern State shirts in the room, but there were none.

"Well, look who is here, Daniel Simmons!" David said.

Daniel, who had been on his phone, looked up to see his old friend.

"David! I was hoping to run into you. How's it going?" Daniel asked.

"I'm doing fine. You?"

"I'm good." Daniel replied, "I'll be even better if we can get Charlie Gray to sign with us."

"Trust me, I've done my part in trying to sway him." David said with a laugh.

The Clear View Principal stood before the crowd of people to get their attention and let them know the event was starting. David turned to look at the Principal and realized that he needed to stand beside the table beside where Marshal Lee was already in place.

He told Daniel, "I'll be right back." as he walked over to the table.

The three players already wearing their new school's gear looked on as Charlie Gray was about to make his decision.

"I'm happy to announce that I will be signing and committing to Henderson University." Charlie said as he picked up and put on the hat with the Henderson logo.

The crowd of people watching cheered as David managed to put on a proud smile, even though his smile was not very convincing. The four who sat at the table then picked up their pens and each signed their letters of intent at the same time. After those in attendance got their many pictures of the players behind the table, it was announced that refreshments would be served. As everyone flocked to the food table, David made his way back to Daniel who stood awkwardly closer to the exit.

"Well, I tried." David said to him with disappointment.

"Hey, it happens. Our program, as you know, is in need of a reboot." Daniel replied.

"Is it just you that is here from the school?" David asked.

"Yes, and I'm on staff with the athletic department, not basketball."

"I've noticed things aren't looking so good over there. That's a shame." David said.

Daniel explained, "Yeah, as I'm sure you've heard, we're in between coaches. We thought we'd have somebody by now, but the interview process has been rough." he continued. "We've got all the right pieces there already, but that's nothing without leadership."

"You're right about that." David replied.

"I'm surprised we even made it to Charlie's final two schools. We've already lost a few commitments this year."

David responded, "If it makes you feel any better, I'm pretty sure that I'll know how the whole reboot thing feels around here next season."

"What if it's not here?" Daniel asked.

Suddenly intrigued, David asked curiously, "I'm sorry?"

"David, we've all been impressed with what you've done in your time as head coach."

David glanced over to his four former players that just signed and then replied with a smile, "Well, thank you. I'm glad my work is acknowledged by you fine people at ESU."

Knowing where the conversation was headed, David thought it was necessary and felt comfortable talking himself up and taking full credit. It did not matter that he was in the same room as the ones it was truly owed to.

"I think I would be able to get you an interview. Is that something you'd be interested in?" Daniel asked.

David paused for a moment and pretended to think the question through while the voice in his head immediately screamed *Yes! Of course!*

He played it cool and in a calm manner replied, "I'd sure have a hard time saying no to that."

The two acquaintances traded phone numbers and before walking out Daniel said, "I'll see what I can do. We'll be in touch."

"Sounds great, I appreciate it." said David, feeling elated and relieved that a door to the perfect situation suddenly had a chance of being opened. Aside from placing all of his hopes on it, his attention was instantly focused on the opportunity that had come out of nowhere. David stood there and looked down at Daniel's business card that he held in his hand. He took out his phone and entered the number feeling that he was creating a new and very important contact. David was standing there still focused on his phone when he felt a tap on his shoulder.

"Hey, Coach." said the voice from behind him.

David turned around to see the father of one of the signees.

"Would you like some cake?" the man asked as he held out a paper plate.

"Oh, no. I'm fine, but thanks." David replied, almost forgetting about the occasion and his reason for being there.

Thoughts of the future suddenly gave him a new feeling of intrigue and put an end to his dread of facing it. This was another excuse for David to check out of the real world around him. His habit of being engrossed in circumstances yet to unfold kicked in stronger than ever. It was clear to those around him that his mind was elsewhere; there was no hiding it. It was evident at school throughout the remainder of the school week, but was heightened drastically back at home. The short off-season time that David had each year was always the time Beth looked forward to the most.

Year after year, she had seen the result of her husband's ego and self-absorption grow steadily over time. Now each evening as she observed him, Beth hardly ever saw him without his phone capturing his full attention. Beth was in no way aware of the reason for his sudden interest in his device. He had always been known as a difficult person to reach on his phone. It was usually on silent and put away. Anyone who wanted to reach him had better luck going through Beth, so she often played the role of messenger.

Beth was busy planning Molly's birthday party which was coming up in a few days, but she could not help but notice David's obsession with his phone. Her curiosity grew, but she thought that yet another change in her husband's behavior had happened within the year. Even so, she felt a strong desire to address it. While lying in their dark bedroom, the only light came from David's screen and shined on his face. After Beth waited for what seemed like forever, David finally reached for his charger, plugged in his phone, and placed it on the nightstand.

As soon as he laid back down, Beth asked, "What's going on?"

"What's going on? What do you mean?" David replied.

"The phone. Just last week you acted like you could barely work it; now you can't keep your eyes off the thing." she said.

After a few seconds of silence, David knew he had to share the news that he was still keeping to himself.

"Okay, look." he said, "You remember my college friend, Daniel Simmons?"

"Um, yes. I think so." Beth replied, wondering where this was going.

"Well, he works for the ESU Athletic Department now, and I happened to run into him at the signing earlier this week. He mentioned a possible interview for their head basketball coach position."

"And he wants you to interview for it?" she asked.

"Yes … me. He gave me his number, and I'm so worried I'll miss his call. You know how I am. If I miss it, I may not get another one." he said in a tone that pleaded for empathy.

While David explained himself, Beth could only think of the difficulty that the opportunity could bring. She disregarded the many steps that still had to be taken and jumped to the possibility of him accepting the job.

"That's big. Why didn't you tell me?" Beth asked.

"Well, in case there actually ends up being no interview. I just really wanted to be sure before …"

"But what if there is one?" she asked, breaking him off. "Were you even going to tell me then?"

"Of course!" he assured her.

"What if you do get the job? I'm sure you've thought of that possibility." Beth said, "Do you know what that would do to your family? We'd have to move hours away. I mean, what about your two children?"

As David listened to the endless questions from Beth that began with the word "what", he began to feel fed up with her questions. He was in no way surprised at her reaction, which was the main reason he had kept the news to himself. David had had enough, and he rolled over.

With his back to her, David told Beth, "We'll talk about this later. Now's not the time."

"There is no "later" ... we can no longer avoid these things! You have to face reality."

"Whatever you say, Beth." David replied halfheartedly as he closed his eyes.

Beth's heart pounded while lying there wide awake replaying the longest conversation she had had with her husband in a long time. She realized the only reason David had bothered to talk that much was because the subject was on him. The price that came along with her speaking up was more clarity about the truth. Beth found herself wishing that what had been unknown by her could have just stayed that way. A whole new problem came crashing down on the many others that she was already dealing with ... and had been dealing with for years. Beth had come to the conclusion that there was not much hope of her husband making any changes. What was next, she didn't know. What she did know was that she would have to do what was best for the children and her own good. She really hoped that it would not get to that point, but only time would soon tell.

Chapter 8

Days later

David had given his word and made his choice. The name he anticipated seeing on his phone screen for days appeared, and the interview was a full go. There was no turning back now that he was on a path that fully diverted his attention from Beth and his kids. This seemed obvious as he had watched them drive away just moments earlier. Time was of the essence. He had to be on his way as soon as possible. After hanging up the phone, David quickly headed back inside to change clothes. Scanning his closet trying to find the right shirt to wear, he slid the hangers back and forth with no luck in doing so. David had never taken much interest in his attire, after all Beth had always chosen his shirts. That was his first realization that he had taken some parts of their relationship for granted.

At that moment, he could not help but think of the implications of what had just happened. Burning in his mind was the sight of Beth's car fading into the distance with their kids in it. However, he thought to himself, *Stop it! It's too late now.* He knew there was simply no time to get caught up in that kind of thinking right now.

When he looked at the many options of shirts from which he had to choose, each one looked the same from his distracted perspective. As he was about to give up on his search for the proper attire, he pulled his phone out again. He looked at his most recent calls list and tapped on Daniel's name. After ringing a few times, Daniel's voice sounded on the other end.

"Hello?"

"Daniel, it's David here again."

"Hey, David. Are you on the way?" Daniel asked.

"Not yet, I was just wondering what I need to wear?" David asked with slight embarrassment.

Daniel responded straightforwardly, "Man, just grab some nice shirts and come on. You can change at my place right here by the school."

"Oh, alright." David replied.

"Yeah, I'll send you the address and will meet you there." said Daniel.

"Sounds good, I'm headed there now."

David put his phone back into his black gym shorts pocket and randomly selected three dress shirts, a pair of black dress pants and black shoes. With his hands full of clothes hangers, David was out the door and to his truck. After hanging the shirts in the backseat, David got in and started the truck, setting the air conditioning on full blast. Before backing out of the driveway, he took a moment to process all that had just happened. He was about to leave for a chance at his dream job, yet the delight he had anticipated having at such a time was replaced with a sense of disgrace. He knew the events of the few moments before receiving the long-awaited call was the cause of those feelings.

As David began the long drive, he sensed a feeling of less remorse about Beth's major decision. The more he thought about it, he nearly decided that he did not even mind that it had happened. He did, however, mind *when* it happened. At the worst possible time ever!! He ultimately, in his mind, decided that there was not too much to what had transpired.

To himself, David thought, *She'll be back. All three of them will be.*

He convinced himself that the sole purpose of the scene Beth had made by leaving was to send a message and get his attention, but what it had actually done, in his mind, was spoil his special moment. As he drove along the highway listening to sports radio, David decided that he would not let the significance of this job opportunity be overshadowed by her actions. He drilled the thought "*it's no big deal*" in his mind. He felt certain that his family would be waiting for him when he returned home. That notion allowed him to look ahead and think of other things.

David had made the trip to and from the ESU campus countless times before. He realized that none of those trips were quite like the one he found himself on now. The drive to the university had much more emotional weight than the ones to the frequent football games that he had attended and the few basketball games that he had been able to squeeze into his schedule. He was now on the way to something that he never could have anticipated happening.

As he neared the school, David turned the radio down and took in his surroundings. When he entered the college town, memories came flooding back in ways that they never had before. Though there had been a rush to make it to the interview, David felt the urge to just slow down and take it all in. He leisurely drove along the downtown streets and seemed to experience a feeling of timelessness as he continued to reminisce on simpler times. The setting looked much different, having grown substantially over the years with newer buildings and developments. Despite that, the feeling that it gave him had not changed since his days as a student there many years ago. It was a similar emotion that he used to have every morning when he got out of bed … the belief that he could do anything. He envisioned how things once were, not only in the town but also in his own life, and how far life had pushed him away from better days.

David now felt closer than he had in years to what he viewed as his prime. He took a much needed moment to ease his mind and clear his thoughts. He didn't want any distractions to keep him from being his best self. However, he soon found his mind totally swirling again. After driving down every street imaginable in the downtown area, he entered the address Daniel had sent him, 111 Elm Street, into the GPS on his phone. David drove ahead and soon reached Elm Street. It was only a few blocks away from the school. He passed the houses in the suburban neighborhood and saw the many children outside in the yards and along the sidewalks enjoying a warm Saturday afternoon in late Spring.

"Your destination is on your left." said the automated voice on his phone as he neared the end of Elm Street. Seeing the mailbox that had the numbers "111" on it, David pulled his truck in front of it and parked alongside the street curb. He heard the instantly recognizable sound of a basketball bouncing when he opened his door. After getting out of his truck, he opened the back door and looked straight ahead through the window on the other side. Near the house he saw a young boy in Daniel's driveway shooting a basketball. David grabbed the clothes hangers and began walking toward the boy. Seeing the stranger approaching, the boy stopped dribbling the ball and bluntly asked, "Who are you?"

"I'm David Jackson, here to meet Daniel Simmons."

"Oh." the boy said as he continued dribbling, "That's my dad."

"Is your dad inside?" David asked.

The boy continued his shot as he replied, "Nope. He had to go to work today, of course."

"Oh, okay." David replied as he watched the ball bounce off of the rim.

It became clear to David that the boy had no intention of further conversation, so he asked him,

"So you're a basketball player, huh?"

"Yeah." the boy replied, "My dad was too."

"Oh, I know. I played with him." David said.

Instead of shooting the basketball again, the boy turned around as his eyes lit up. He suddenly became interested in David even though he was still a strange man who he had never seen before.

"Really?" the boy enthusiastically asked David.

"Yeah, really! We played at ESU, right down the road from here," David replied.

"That's where he works now." the boy said.

David said, "I know, that's where I'm hoping to …"

"He's back!" the boy yelled as he dropped the ball and ran toward his father's car as it pulled into the driveway.

David was taken aback by the boy's obvious fascination and love for his dad. Such emotion had never been present with his own father. Nor was it with his son, Elijah. Both were equally complicated relationships.

Daniel got out of his car and met his son with open arms as he bent down to embrace him.

"Hey, buddy." he said to the boy.

Saying the words David had always hoped to hear his son say, the boy asked, "Dad, can we play a one-on-one game?"

"Just one second." he said as he looked over to David. "I'm surprised this guy right here hasn't challenged you yet." Daniel said with a laugh.

He then looked back to his son and said, "I have to show Mr. David where to change his clothes. I guess you two met?"

"Oh yeah, I met the ball player." David said with a smile.

"Did you have a good trip?" Daniel asked as he walked over to David.

"I did. It's always nice to be back at ESU." David replied.

"Well, I'll walk you inside. Just come back through this way when you're finished."

"Sounds good." said David.

"I'll be right back!" Daniel said as he turned toward to his son.

The two walked inside through the garage and were greeted by Daniel's wife when they entered the house.

"Honey, you remember David, don't you?" Daniel asked her.

"Oh, of course!" she replied, remembering the days where she too attended ESU with them.

"You've hardly changed at all from college!" she said with a laugh.

As the comment boosted him, David modestly replied, "Ha, I don't know about that."

"She tells me that every morning just so I'll get out of bed." Daniel said to him, joining in the laughter.

"How's your wife? Beth is it?" she asked.

"Oh, yeah. That's her. She's good … yeah. Doing good." David stumbled while replying to what was once a simple question to answer.

"I remember sitting with her in the stands during so many games back in the day. Tell her I said hello!"

"Will do." David replied.

After spending most of the drive pushing the thought of her aside, Beth was back on his mind. The sudden boost David had gotten from the light hearted chatter was now gone and replaced with that same dispirited feeling he had earlier.

"The bathroom is the second door down that hallway." Daniel said as he pointed in its direction. He continued, "I guess I'll be outside playing a quick one on one."

Daniel then opened the door and headed out for a quick game with his son. With the hangers in one hand, dress pants and shoes in the other, David walked down the hall and into the bathroom. He flipped on the light, closed the door, and randomly selected a shirt from the several he brought along to wear. No longer in the mood to impress, the pressure that had weighed on him earlier, was no longer what was on his mind. It was evident to him now that the weight of despair was much heavier than any other pressure he had ever experienced. While buttoning his shirt, David looked at his reflection in the mirror. He stared deep into his own eyes and saw the loneliness that he had pretended not to feel. He flashed a big smile in an attempt to erase the despondent image, but it could do nothing but fade away.

David took a few more minutes to finish getting dressed and then walked out with his hands full. When Daniel's wife saw him, she immediately walked over to the door that led to the garage and opened it for him.

"I appreciate it." David said.

"Of course!" she replied with a big smile, "It was great seeing you."

As David walked down the steps, he could hear the ball bouncing yet again from the driveway. He could also hear two voices in the mix. While walking through the garage, he saw a likeness of what he had always dreamed of being. The sight of a father and son playing the sport that he loved more than anything brought a soft smile to David's face. Watching Daniel pretend to guard his son while he dribbled the ball to make a lay-up lifted his thoughts into a realm that he never wanted to leave ... also one he had never been able to call his own.

"Alright!" Daniel told his son, "The next point wins. I've got to head back to work for a little while."

The boy suddenly stopped, and the look on his face showed his disappointment.

"You're going back?" he asked his dad.

"Well, yeah. I need to introduce Mr. David for his interview."

The boy's eyes slowly turned to look at David, who could only stand and watch as he felt guilty for ending their special time together. Tears began to stream down the boy's face. He was obviously embarrassed to cry in front of his father.

Daniel bent down, put his hand on his son's shoulder and told him, "I'll be back soon. Now wipe those tears and practice up for the next game."

The boy lifted his head and listened to his dad. With the basketball in one hand, he used his other to wipe his face. It pained David to see the young boy upset just moments after witnessing him experiencing pure joy. He was never one for awkward situations; and whenever tears were involved, he never knew how to react. To David, it appeared Daniel had everything in complete control. The uncomfortable moment ended when he reached down and gave his son a big hug. It seemed to be all the signal that the boy needed to know that everything was okay and he needed to toughen up.

Daniel stood up and began walking to his car at the end of the driveway.

"Alright, let's roll." he told David, who then followed along.

David could not resist the urge to turn around and look at the boy who was watching the two of them walk away.

"Nice to meet you. I don't think I got your name?" David said after Daniel got into the car. The boy did not respond except with a look of resentment as he turned around and continued dribbling the basketball alone. David was able to do nothing but cringe with a feeling of embarrassment. Daniel already had his car started. As David neared it, he put the window down.

"I'll meet you over at the athletic offices, you know where that is, right?" Daniel asked.

David, in an uneasy and shaken tone responded, "Uh, yeah. I think so."

While he continued walking to his truck, he could not help but think of how Daniel made leaving his son look effortless, like it was merely routine. For the first time, David was beginning to truly question how he, himself, interacted with his own family. There was no correlation he could make between his own life and what he had just experienced in Daniel's household. It seemed very different from the one he went to and from every day. Yet, there was one connection that could be made. The connection was not with

Daniel as a father, but with the boy as a son.

As David got into his truck, he looked over toward the young boy once again. This time it was as if he was looking at a spitting image of himself at that age. He thought back to the many days he had spent in his own driveway with a ball in hand hoping that his father would come home. David remembered that the waiting was painful. Most of the afternoons ended with darkness covering the sky and his mother's voice calling him inside … day after day without his dad in sight. The reality of it all lay heavy on David as he pulled his truck away from the curb feeling empathy in a way he never had before.

He followed closely behind Daniel on the short drive to the ESU campus. As they turned into the main entrance, David realized that the interview was the furthest thing from his mind. He pulled into the parking lot alongside a limited number of vehicles. Taking his time to get out of his truck, Daniel had walked on ahead of him. Trying to clear his mind and get focused on his reason for being there, he got out of his vehicle, straightened his tie, and took a deep breath before walking to the steps of the main athletic offices. The significance of the moment was still not on his mind as he made his way into the lobby and saw Daniel waiting for him.

"I'll go tell our AD, Mr. Cunningham, that you have arrived." said Daniel. "You can wait over there if you'd like." he said, pointing to a set of couches and chairs.

"Before you do that, I need to tell you something." David said walking closer to Daniel.

"Alright." Daniel replied.

"I'm so sorry you had to leave your son to come set this thing up. It means a lot."

"No worries." Daniel said as he began to walk away.

"And another thing." said David as he reached his hand out to stop Daniel. "How do you make doing such a thing look so easy?"

"Look." Daniel said, giving David a look of annoyance, "It's the hardest thing in the world. After I say goodbye each day, I have to keep walking because I know if I turn around to see the look on his face, there would be no chance I could leave him."

Before David could say anything more, Daniel continued, "You're right. I set this thing up for you today, and I don't need to be embarrassed. This is a big opportunity for you; and it seems to me that your head isn't in the right space, so go walk around for a minute and get it there."

David nodded his head and took a few steps back as Daniel walked toward the athletic director's office. The fact that he did not want to waste Daniel's time was now at the forefront of his thoughts. David knew he needed to do whatever it took not to do so. He was unable to think of the first part of Daniel's response from a father's perspective as the pressure to be the champion coach was back on. David knew he needed to make a good impression. Now he had just a short few moments to get his thoughts settled and focused. He wanted to live up to Daniel's expectations ... and his own, for that matter.

Instead of staying in the lobby, David walked over to the Trophy Room. He thought perhaps a revisit to the times in his life when he had experienced a sense of gratification would get him in the right frame of mind for his interview. He walked around looking at former ESU basketball team photos and memorabilia. As he viewed the displays, his thoughts went back in time. He examined the aligned photos ranging from the school's first ever team to its most recent one. Only about half of them were actually printed in color. David scanned the photos taken at center court each year. He looked for the early nineties section which marked his era as an ESU basketball player. He hoped that at least one of the four photos he was in would be in color. Making it to that section of the display, he saw that there were actually *two*. David felt a little less old, but he could not help but notice nearly thirty other team photos followed behind his freshman year.

Under that particular season's picture, the frame read "1991-92". David was immediately able to spot himself seated among the other shorter players on the front row. Sitting two seats from him was Daniel Simmons. Seeing Daniel's picture reminded him that his reason for being in that room was to get himself together, and he only had a few minutes left to do so. David looked back at his own photo again. There he was with the number 14 on his jersey and his thick long hairstyle matching many of the others in the photo. The bright smile he was flashing in the photo was a true representation of the beginning of a major high period in his life. It was as if the younger David Jackson already knew what was ahead in his college career.

At only eighteen years old, he had a beautiful fiancé by his side. She had sacrificed going to an ivy league school in order to be with him and watch him follow his dreams. At the same time, David was already making connections at Eastern State in hopes of regaining the same "big man on campus" title he had carried all through high school.

Just you wait, David thought to himself while continuing to look at his eighteen-year-old self ... thinking of all the possibilities that would be in store.

He shifted his eyes over to two other photos in the display. It was the first ever ESU team picture made in full color. That itself was a great portrayal of the significant rise of both the team and of its point guard, David Jackson. After two seasons of limited playing time and limited success for the team, it had finally been David's turn to show if he lived up to his major self-promotion around the school campus. The two years prior to the 1993-94 season were in no way a waste for David as he had learned a lot about college basketball. It was all thanks to the man he always eyed from his seat on the bench during the games ... Head Coach Don Smith. With his newly gained knowledge of the ins and outs of basketball, along with his increasing high standing on campus, life had been good.

The team had made a major transformation and saw success that no ESU basketball team had ever before seen. Game after game, David Jackson led his team to new heights with over ten assists averaged per game. After the many wins and the few occasional losses, his fiancé, Beth, was the first to tell David how proud she was of him. Working her way through college and heading toward graduate school, Beth had always taken the time to support him even though she was heavily engrossed in her studies.

In those moments of reflection, David continued to stare at his younger self in the photo. He felt as if he was that twenty-year-old young man once again. It seemed that he had been transported back in time. He was so lost in memories that he had not heard the sound of Daniel's voice from the doorway.

"David!" Daniel repeated louder as he walked closer to him.

David turned around in surprise.

"He's ready for you." said Daniel, "Are *you* ready?"

David stood silent for a moment and then smiled in a way that resembled the ones in all four of his team pictures

In a refreshed state of mind, David replied in a manner and with words that his younger, dramatic self would have said, "I think I was born ready."

Chapter 9

David felt self-assured as he followed Daniel to the end of the long hallway. On both sides were offices of the athletic department staff. As they approached the last door on the right, Daniel stepped aside and extended his arm for David to enter first. David noticed the nameplate on the ajar door that read *"B. Cunningham: Athletic Director"* as he strolled into the office as if it were his own. Directly in front of him was a desk in the center of the spacious room. A large office chair was behind it but was turned backward. All he could see was its purple leather which matched the school's colors. While Daniel remained near the doorway, David stood near the desk with his hand on the back of one of the two smaller chairs that were in front of it. They both waited for a moment as they heard the sound of a television emanating from behind the chair.

"Mr. Cunningham." Daniel said to get the athletic director's attention.

As the chair quickly turned around, Mr. Cunningham appeared before them.

"Oh, sorry about that, fellas. I was just catching a bit of *Sports Center*." he said as he stood up from his seat. "You must be David Jackson." Mr. Cunningham said as he reached his hand toward David.

"That's me." David replied while shaking his hand.

"I'm Ben Cunningham. Very glad we could squeeze this meeting in at the last second."

"I'll let you two get started." Daniel said as he began to close the door.

"Thank you, Daniel." Mr. Cunningham said. Looking back toward David, he said, "Well, take a seat and make yourself comfortable."

David did exactly that as he sat back into the chair and crossed his legs. With the small television behind his desk still on, Mr. Cunningham began to scramble through the papers on his desk. It was clear that he was looking for the remote which David could spot directly in front of him but out of the athletics director's eyesight.

"I swear … I can never find that thing. Give me a second." Mr. Cunningham said as he turned back around.

He was about to stop searching for the remote and manually turn the television off, but David had already reached for it. Before Mr. Cunningham could press the power button on the side of the television, the screen suddenly went black. He turned toward David to see him holding the remote control out toward him.

"Here you go, sir." David said.

Mr. Cunningham replied with a smile, "Sir? I can't be *that* much older than you." He took the remote and placed it beside the T.V. "You can just call me Ben." he continued.

"Whatever makes you comfortable, Ben." David replied with a laugh.

"I'm going to cut right to the chase." Ben said as he leaned back in his chair. "You're an impressive guy, and we've kept our eyes on your program for the past several years. As you can imagine, we like what you've done."

"Well, I do appreciate that." David replied, unsure of what else to say.

"Now tell me David, how would you do the same thing here?" asked Ben.

David thought for a moment as he realized that he was not so sure how he accomplished what he did at Clear View. The only formula for success that David had ever known was having great players on his teams. Saying, "Well, hopefully I'll have good players here too." as an answer that really did not cut it during an interview for a head coaching position. What he needed to do was dig deep for a response that would not be forgotten.

David replied, "This is home … just like Clear View. There is just something about being home that makes coaching more important than wins and losses. It's about having pride for the place you love, you know?"

Ben nodded his head in response as he was simply enthralled by David's words.

In an impassioned tone, David continued, "Having that pride leads to a totally unmatched passion that can take any team a long way."

As David heard himself say those words, he realized how much true passion he lacked in his life. Any pride that he had was not from representing a place he considered home. His pride had come from the winning itself, as there was nothing else in life that he loved more. The awareness that he was known as a winner had become his sole purpose for enthusiastically getting up every morning to go to a job that built on that identity. The new opportunity had nothing to do with being at another place that he could call home. It was about continuing a legacy that he feared would end if he remained where he was. He wasn't even sure he knew what home really meant anymore, as his own was in pieces. Despite all of that, Ben Cunningham bought every word that David had said.

The interview slowly turned into a conversation between the two men when Ben said, "Speaking of home, I guess I'll forgive you for beating up on my alma mater, Ridgewood High, in the championship game."

"Ridgewood, huh? I'll have to say they're a good team, they gave us a fight." David replied.

"Oh, I was there to see it. That's what caught my attention. Your team made it look effortless out there, and it all starts with you, right?" Ben said.

David, hesitant to respond at first, gave an assuring answer, "No doubt, I'm glad *we* made it seem easy. It surely wasn't."

"But I'll tell ya." David continued as he leaned forward, "It was worth it."

"See, that's the kind of mentality we need around here. I just wish you could've let ole Ridgewood know the feeling of a championship win." Ben said with a laugh.

David leaned back and shrugged his shoulders, "Well, I guess I thought that winning three would feel better than giving up one."

Ben replied with a chuckle, "I tell you what, that's what I'm talking about." he said as he pointed at David, "A winner."

He continued, "A lot has changed since my time there. We sure came nowhere close to a championship when I suited up."

Seeing that Ben did not seem to fit the image of ever having been an athlete, David asked with intrigue, "You played?"

It was a question that led to nearly an hour of time spent swapping basketball stories, which Ben seemed more than willing to share. David soon regretted even asking. He was not aware that Ben was now beginning to view him more as a new friend than as a coaching candidate. His personable quality that seemed so genuine had been fully received by Ben. David's main goal when he had first walked into the office was to take control of the mood. In the middle of hearing countless stories in which he pretended have an interest, David was simply losing control. He had misinterpreted Ben Cunningham's business-like persona. It was a cover-up to the athletic director's ability to endlessly ramble on and on in conversation.

Only Daniel Simmons would be able to save David from the talk fest. While he waited in his office, Daniel got ahead on the next week's work and began looking at tape for future basketball recruits. He glanced at the time on his computer and realized that it was past time for the interview to be completed. Wondering if David was still in Ben's office, he stood up from his desk. The last thing that he wanted to do was spend any extra meaningless time at work on a Saturday. Daniel walked out of his office and locked the door. He had a feeling that David's interview had been long over and he would be waiting for him. He knew that none of the previous interviews had come close to lasting this long. As he neared the athletic director's office, he could hear a voice chatting behind the closed door. When he got closer, he leaned his ear against the door and realized Ben was doing all the talking. It sounded as if he was alone and was simply just shooting the bull over the telephone.

Daniel did not have time for this. He looked down at his watch and could just feel the afternoon with his son fading away. After a few minutes, he knocked on the door. Ben Cunningham's voice paused and said, "Oh. Uh, come on in."

When Daniel opened the door, the look of relief on David's face was the first thing he noticed. Feeling suffocated as Ben had gotten even closer to him by sitting on the front of his desk, David remained seated in the chair. "Daniel! What's going on?" Ben asked.

"Hey, you guys finished up? If so, I think I'll head on home." said Daniel.

Unaware of how much time had gone by, Ben looked at his watch with surprise. "Well would you look at that! Yeah, I think we're all finished up in here. Head on home."

Well aware of how much time had gone by since entering the office, David felt as if he could finally take a deep breath as Ben stood up and took a few steps back.

Ben then reached his hand out and said, "It was a pleasure to meet you. I'm looking forward to the future."

"The pleasure is all mine." David replied as he got up from his seat and shook Ben's hand. "Thank you for meeting with me."

As David was walking toward the door, he heard Ben's voice, "Hey, David."

David turned around to see Ben pointing at him. "We'll be in touch soon."

With a smile, David replied, "Sounds good."

While he was glad to be leaving the office, there was also a feeling of thrill that he felt in his soul. Though his appeal had caused an excessive showing of interest, David had the strong belief that there was no way Ben would choose anyone else to fill the vacant head coaching position.

"I'll see you Monday." Daniel said to Ben; and after getting out into the hallway, he asked David, "So, how'd it go?"

As the two began to slowly walk toward the other end of the long hallway, David replied confidently, "I think it's safe to say that my chances are pretty high."

Thinking of what he had just gone through to feel that way, David felt that it now seemed worth it.

Daniel replied, "Yeah, I'd say your chances are high. I've never heard Ben talk that much to anyone before."

After the two of them shared a laugh, Daniel suddenly had an idea. He checked the time yet again and figured that there were a few extra minutes he could spare before heading home.

As they were exiting the athletic office's main doors, he asked David,

"Before you make the drive back, would you like to stop by the basketball arena and see the facilities?"

David quickly responded, "Would I? Of course! It's been quite some time since I made my way around there."

As they left the building and walked down the front steps, Daniel told him, "I'll meet you over there."

David got back into his truck and had to pause for a moment to enjoy the feeling that all the right pieces were falling into place. He made his way to the arena, which was only two buildings over from the offices. David parked beside Daniel in another near-empty parking lot as most were on campus during a late Saturday afternoon at that time of year. He got out of the truck and walked closer for a better view. He was immediately blown away by the newly remodeled basketball facility that was connected to the arena. David's fascination continued upon entering the building. It was almost unrecognizable from what he remembered from his last visit. Daniel led the way through the building and into the new state-of-the-art locker room. David thought back to the shape it was in during his time on the team.

"These players nowadays just don't know how good they have it, do they?" he said aloud to Daniel as he made his way to where his old locker had been.

"You got that right!" Daniel responded.

"I mean; I've never before been in a locker room that actually smells good." David said with amazement.

Daniel replied, "Don't go falling in love with the locker room. What would be your very own space is in the next room over."

They left the locker room and walked into that very space that Daniel had just mentioned. The sign beside the door, which read "*Coach's Office*" was an understatement. A more accurate term for the room would have been "Coach's Suite." Almost as large as Ben Cunningham's office, the room was nearly empty. Only a large desk and chair filled the space. A large ESU logo hung on the wall. David walked into the office and took a seat in the chair behind the desk. He leaned back and kicked his feet up on the desk as he said, "I could get used to this."

Daniel, observing David's assertiveness and swagger, responded, "You'll have plenty of time to do that. The best part of the tour is down the hall."

David stood up quickly. He knew exactly to what he was referring. He followed Daniel down the hallway which grew larger the farther they walked. It broadened into a tunnel which led to the basketball court. Daniel moved aside to let David take it all in. As he walked onto the court, David imagined the empty arena being filled with fans on game day. He could imagine the sound of their cheers in his mind. Among the many transformations that had been made to the facilities, the arena was the one thing that had remained the same. The large new scoreboard and other improvements that had been made over the years did nothing to change the feeling of walking onto that court.

David made his way to the home bench area beside the score table. That was the spot where he could eventually pace back and forth during the games while coaching his team. He then slowly walked toward the large ESU logo at half-court. David stood still and slowly lifted his head to observe the view from the exact center of the arena. He had been on the court countless times before as a player for the many conditioning workouts, practices, and games. Despite those past experiences, David was dealing with an entirely new perspective. This one allowed him to fully grasp the magnitude of what seemed to be a guaranteed next chapter for him. It was at that moment and in that place that David Jackson realized everything in his life had come full circle.

Chapter 10

Beth Jackson awoke from her nap to realize that it was late afternoon. As she sat up, her mind went back to the reality that she had hoped was just a bad dream. She stood up from the bed in the bedroom where she had slept in her youth. After opening the curtains, Beth looked through the large window. The landscape outside was beautifully highlighted by the bright sun. However, what she saw was the last thing on her mind. As she stared deeply, it all became a blur, and Beth suddenly remembered to blink her burning eyes. She turned around and looked back at the room that the natural light from outside had exposed. Seeing her large over-packed bag on the floor, she was not sure how long her stay would be. The uncertainty about what would come next was already driving her crazy. The one thing that became clear to Beth was how everything had come full circle in her life. It was a much different feeling than her husband had as his dream unfolded before him. For her, it was a lifestyle that she would never have wanted, and was more like a nightmare than a dream come true.

Beth glanced up into a thick gold framed picture her parents had hung over her bed. She saw herself twenty years younger in the wedding dress of her dreams. She walked closer and examined the picture carefully. The bright smile she saw there had become harder to show as the years had gone by. Even though many life experiences had led up to this moment, the changes in her relationship with David still felt so sudden to her. She paused to think about the big decision that had been looming in her mind for quite some time. The wedding picture sent Beth back to that very day, and she wondered just how disappointed her younger self would be if she had known how life would eventually turn out. In the picture, Beth noticed the ring that had just been placed on her finger. She then looked down at her hand to see the same ring she had worn every day since. Even after all of the years, it still looked brand new; but she was not sure what it represented anymore. There was a lot about which Beth was now unsure.

As she turned and looked around her old bedroom, she realized it had hardly changed at all from her teenage years; it was clear the journey of life had led her back to where she started. The wallpaper remained the same. The old telephone and alarm clock beside her bed were still there. Her many cheer trophies lined the shelves. Beth felt as if she had been transported back in time to those days. She wished she could relive the carefree feelings of that part of her life. It had included a wide array of hopes and dreams that were now in danger of being lost. As she heard the sounds of Elijah and Molly's laughter in the other room, Beth felt assurance that she would always have what she considered to be her greatest joys in life. Hearing the kids allowed Beth to quickly reassess where she was in life. The stay away from home, she thought, would be seen as going back to the drawing board. It would allow her to gain control of a situation that had nearly pushed her over the edge. She knew there were two choices. She could either fall off the edge or draw on her strength to push back even harder.

As soon as Beth opened her bedroom door, the familiar aroma of her mother's cooking filled the air. While taking it in, she knew there was nothing she needed more than a home- cooked meal. Beth walked down the dark hallway and heard the voices from the kitchen area grow louder. Before rounding the corner, she paused for a moment and peeked ahead at the loving sight in front of her. It was no wonder why both Elijah and Molly were laughing so much. Seeing her father sitting across from the two of them at the table, Beth had her answer. The smile on Elijah's face in particular caught her attention as she saw him respond to the attention his grandad lovingly gave to him during each visit.

"There she is!" Beth's father said as she entered the kitchen.

"Just in time." her mother said while getting plates from the cabinet.

Beth smiled while her eyes adjusted to the brighter lights in the room and then replied, "Wow, looks like it." as she glanced over at the food while taking her seat beside her father.

"Elijah do you mind getting the forks and knives for me? Molly, how about you get some napkins for us?" her mother asked.

The kids got up from their seats and did their part in helping set up the table.

"Is there anything I can do, Mom?" Beth asked.

"The only thing I can think of is to get ready for some of my famous pork chops." her mother replied with a smile.

Beth's parents always enjoyed having their only two grandchildren over for weekend stays. Only half an hour away, their door was always open to the frequent visits from Beth's family, and they were happy to host them for any meal or occasion. It was no secret to them that this visit was unlike any other. It had been clear to them when they saw the overnight bag that Beth carried for herself. Still, they asked no questions after learning that Beth would also be staying over. They were well aware of the struggles in their daughter's marriage, and they had seen less of their son-in-law as time had gone by. Beth always did her best to brush things aside around her parents, pretending things were okay. As they began to eat, Beth acted as if things were normal; but by the time the meal was completed, she had grown silent. Her father took control of the conversation and kept the kids in good spirits while eating dessert, but her mother found it impossible to ignore the obvious.

While the kids moved their plates aside and set up a board game on the table, Beth's mother stood up and began to gather everything from the table.

As Beth watched her father explaining the rules of the game to the kids, her mother's eyes were focused on her. She knew her daughter well enough to know that something was heavy on her mind. Speaking in a soft voice, she said, "Beth, do you mind giving me a hand with the dishes?" She was hoping to gain some assurance of her daughter's well-being.

Beth nodded and gathered a handful of plates to take into the kitchen. When joining her mother, she said, "Do you still go through this much trouble every night?"

"Yes, every night. Unless your father treats me to dinner. But I enjoy it." she replied.

They could hear the laughter from the table. Looking back toward them, Beth enjoyed seeing the kids laughing and happy, thanks to the entertainment from their granddad.

"He's always been so good with kids." Beth said as she cleaned off a plate.

"Oh yes. They're good for him." her mother replied.

"And he's even better for them, trust me." said Beth.

Her mother paused for a moment as the water continued to run into the sink. She then said, "You don't have to tell me anything else, all I care about is that you're okay. Are you?"

Without any hesitation, Beth replied, "I'm fine mom, really. I am."

Her mother, really wanting to believe what Beth had said, stood quietly for a moment before she responded, "Well you know you are free to stay as long as you'd like."

"I think it'll just be for a night or two. It's nothing more than needing to reset." Beth said as she avoided looking directly at her mother.

Her mother replied with a smile, "Well, there's no better place than home to do just that." She felt a little better about Beth's circumstances, but was not fully convinced that all was well.

For David, the time to reset had yet to begin. After his quick walk through all of the basketball facilities, Daniel Simmons insisted that David join him for dinner to celebrate his seemingly good chances of being hired. David was a bit hesitant to accept the offer. "Ah, come on." Daniel said. "Since you're already here, we could go to any of the best spots downtown. My treat." Hearing the latter remark intrigued David and made the offer even harder to decline.

"Well, if you insist." David replied with a smile.

"Great! I think I know the perfect place." Daniel said as they left the arena and headed back to their parked cars. "You can just leave your car here, and we'll swing by to get it later on."

When they reached the parking lot, the two of them got in Daniel's car.

Before starting the car, Daniel pulled out his phone, "Let me call the wife and tell her I'll be a bit late tonight." "Now you know I can't hang out as late as I used to back in the good ole days." David said with a laugh and without ever thinking of Daniel's son who was still bouncing the basketball in anticipation of his father's car pulling back into the driveway.

After Daniel's quick phone conversation with his wife, the two were off and made their way to the downtown area. That began several hours of continuing to relive and reminisce their college days while visiting all of the classic hot spots around the college town. Their chatting throughout the entire evening was not about anything very personal. It was more about basketball. Their memories from times together with the team led to many laughs. They both eventually saw the same tired look in the other and knew it was time to call it a day. Daniel drove David back to his truck in the parking lot, and they casually said goodbye with the expectation of seeing each other again very soon.

"Once you're down here full time, we'll have to make this a once a week thing." Daniel said as David got out of his car.

"Sounds good to me. I'm looking forward to it." David replied.

"I don't know about you, but I'm feeling really old right now." said Daniel from his rolled down window as he began to drive away.

"It's not just you." David replied with a laugh while opening his truck door.

After starting his engine, David leaned his head back and closed his eyes for a moment. It was impossible to recap everything that he had encountered in one single day, and the day was not over. There was still a lengthy drive back home for him. Only with the help of a cold Mountain Dew and the radio on full blast would he be able to remain awake during the drive home. Even though he was completely exhausted, David felt complete and his spirits were high. His failure to see his life outside of a compartmentalized view led him to feel that way. Deep down inside he knew there was a much bigger issue brewing, but this was his day. As far as he was concerned, he felt that he had seized it. Any worries would just have to wait until the next day. As he drove along the highway during Saturday's late hours, David was going to enjoy and hold onto the night that he began to wish would never end.

By the end of the drive, there was nothing David could have possibly enjoyed more than pulling into his own driveway and heading straight to bed. The home's sheer emptiness would not hit him until the next morning. When he awoke more than an hour later than usual, he realized just how much he relied on his daily alarm. Even on a Sunday, David managed to start his day at the crack of dawn. As his eyes opened, he found himself directly in the middle of the king-sized bed without Beth who would normally be lying to his right every morning. Instead of concern, he felt an appreciation for the extra space as he stretched his arms and legs out wide. Then the realization that he was behind on his daily routine hit him. He quickly got up to begin his day, and after a quick cup of coffee while checking into what was going on in the world of sports, he headed to the gym as he did every morning.

When his workout was complete, David drove slowly back down the neighborhood street. He noticed something out of the ordinary. When he got within sight of his home, the first thing he saw was Beth's car parked in the driveway. He slowed down and blinked a few times at the sight and how it was almost identical to the previous day ... even to the detail of the car backed close to the front walkway with the trunk opened. David saw the kids carrying their bags up the front steps and into the house. He parked his truck beside Beth's car and just sat there for a moment. He began to brace himself before inevitably getting chewed out. He got out of his truck and started walking slowly toward the opened front door. As he got nearer, more extreme thoughts came to his mind. *Is it my turn to leave for the night? Is she expecting me to pack up? What's going on?*

When David entered the house, everything seemed strangely quiet. Looking around, he was startled at the sight of Beth as he almost bumped into her after entering the kitchen area.

"Oh!" David said with surprise. "Hi there." he continued, unsure of what to expect next.

"Hey!" Beth replied in an oddly upbeat tone. "Would you mind bringing in those bags of groceries from the trunk of my car?"

"Um, yeah. No, I don't mind. Of course." David replied as he backed up in confusion at his wife's mood.

After gathering the bags and taking them into the kitchen where Beth was storing the other groceries, David asked, "So what all did you get?"

"You know, just the usual stuff for the week." Beth replied, "I also got some hamburgers for you to grill later on."

"Oh, yeah. Okay … that sounds good to me." David replied as he walked away with a puzzled expression on his face.

As the day went on, more questions arose in David's mind, but he had no intention of saying them aloud and disturbing the home's strangely calm atmosphere. He decided not to try to fix what appeared to be unbroken, a view he had every reason to believe. Beth did not seem to be in the mood that he had become accustomed to in recent months. He watched her as she moved around and appeared to be more like herself in former days with a less tense outlook on life. He was not quite sure how to feel about it, but he was glad to feel some relief from his perplexity while attempting to comprehend where he stood as a husband. How he had managed to get past what seemed like a dire situation in his marriage, David did not know; but it seemed to him as if he was somehow in the clear.

When dinner time neared, David started the grill in the backyard while Beth sat on the back porch and the kids roamed around together outside. It felt like old times as Elijah and Molly interacted with each other without any form of technology in their hands. While flipping the hamburgers, David kept glancing over to Beth where she sat reading peacefully in the porch swing. There was a look of contentment on her face as if everything in her life was under control. David knew, however, that was likely not the case due to the recent stress she had endured. Obtaining her real estate license while continuing to teach evening math classes at the local community college had led to a nonstop schedule for her. It had begun to feel as if they did better when they each did their own thing. When they were together, the hectic nature of their lives tended to bring out the worst in each of them. As the smoke rose and the smell of charcoal filled the air, David felt a sense of security in the thought that a new page was beginning to turn.

Beth eventually placed her bookmark between the pages and went inside to gather plates and other supplies. She came out with a tray and signaled to the kids that it was time to wash up.

"I thought we could eat out here. We haven't put this picnic table to use in a long time." she told David.

"That's fine with me." David replied as he laid out the plastic tablecloth that Beth had handed to him.

Before Elijah and Molly came back outside, David watched as Beth set the four plates on the table. He noticed the familiar blank look on her face.

Breaking the silence, David said to her, "This was a good idea."

"Mhmm." Beth mumbled as she continued removing items from the tray and remained focused on the table.

When the kids opened the sliding door to come from inside, David noticed Beth's expression change as she perked up and turned around to face them making their way down the porch steps.

"Dinner time!" she declared as David looked on and tried to make sense of the quick shift he had just witnessed.

When they each took their seats, Elijah sat next to Beth and Molly stood still as she looked at the remaining spot beside her dad.

"Mom." she said, "I was going to sit beside you."

"There's plenty of room. Just bring your plate, and we'll slide over." Beth told her.

Even though the seating arrangement said a lot about what their family dynamic had become, David did not give much thought to his daughter's request to sit beside her mother. Even as he found himself alone on one side of the table as his wife and kids stared at him from across it, the pleasant ambience that he had felt that day was not deterred. Beth stayed upbeat and maintained the lighthearted conversation that went on well after they had finished eating. It was unusual for the four of them to be together at the same place for any extended period of time. On the rare occasion when a meal was shared together as a family, it was often done in near silence. It was not until the sunlight started to dim and mosquitos began to swarm that the Jacksons cleared the picnic table and headed inside. After leaving their plates by the kitchen sink, the kids headed straight to their rooms leaving David and Beth alone. Only the sound of running water onto the soiled plates could be heard. Silence had yet again taken over between the two of them.

"Do you need any help?" David apathetically asked as he stood there watching her.

Beth replied with the same lack of enthusiasm as his question by saying, "I've got it *all* under control." with an assuring smile that David mistook as meaningful.

He also saw it as his signal to clear the room, which he was more than willing to do. David sighed in relief after retreating to his recliner and escaping the waves of friction which he realized seemed to come from Beth only when the kids were out of sight. Before reaching over for the television remote control, David did the quick math in his head as he thought of Molly's age. Ten years were left before she would head off to college. *A whole decade!* For a few moments, David thought about it. He felt sure ten years was plenty of time to work things out with Beth before they would become empty nesters. With that in mind, he turned to a major league baseball game. He had once again put the issues plaguing his marriage on hold. For David, steering clear of the long-standing matter to which Beth had become a prisoner was something that he could still afford to do … or so he thought.

Beth heard the sound of the television turn on in the living room. She lowered her head in disappointment. It was the same feeling that she had gotten the day before while looking in the rear-view mirror after leaving home with the kids and three overnight bags in the car. She had done so in hopes of seeing David's truck appear out of nowhere in an all-out chase for the family that he had taken for granted. Instead, she realized that he was going after his own desires- desires that were in the opposite direction.

That night, after tossing and turning in her childhood bed, she had stared out the window as she fantasized David's headlights shining brightly as they appeared in her parents' driveway. She had closed her eyes and imagined the sight of her husband sprinting toward her window only to open them and see the pitch black setting that resembled her soul.

Tonight David was just a room away, but Beth knew there was much more separating them than a single wall. It was an even thicker one that he had built around himself with no way for her to get in. It was the thought of his constant failure to read the signals that she had long been sending to him that brought her to tears yet again. The emotional restraint that she had maintained throughout the day was now gone. Coming back home had been Beth's way of giving one last chance to the man that she still loved. She had desperately hoped that he would make the most of it. Seeing that David had blown his opportunity, Beth felt that there was no more left for her to give.

She quickly got herself together, left the kitchen, and headed straight to the master bedroom. Closing the door behind her, she stood still trying to pull her thoughts together. Her unpacked overnight bag was on the bed where she had left it. Beth wondered if there was any reason to remove the clothes that were in it. She knew that the likelihood of many more of her items being packed up was high. Pushing the bag aside, she sat down on the side of the bed as she pondered the inevitable future. She glanced over at her reflection in the large mirror above the dresser and then shifted her eyes down to the bottom drawer. After taking a deep breath, she stood up, walked over to the bedroom door, and quietly locked it. Walking back to the dresser that she shared with David, Beth's heart began to pound. She knelt down and wiped her sweaty palms off on the carpet before opening the bottom drawer. She knew what was in it would change everything.

Beth pulled the drawer open and began to rummage through some of her miscellaneous items in search of the yellow envelope that she had placed at the very bottom months before. After quietly moving aside other documents, folders, and old jewelry boxes, the yellow envelope appeared face down where its color blended in with the wood on which it had been placed. Beth slowly reached for it and placed it on the bed. Then quickly gathering the items that were strewn out from the drawer, she jammed them back inside of it. She forced the drawer to shut and stood back up to take a closer look at the envelope. Her heart continued to beat at the same rapid pace as she turned it around to see "*Stevenson Family Law*" in large, bold letters.

Over the course of the many long weeks that had passed since requesting the separation papers from her lawyer, Beth had hoped that they could eventually be thrown away. She had held on to the hope that David would make the time to help resolve their issues once the intense basketball season ended. Her optimism had now faded away, and there was nothing left for her to do but resort to a different resolution of their issues in order to prevent any further self-destruction. Beth placed the envelope on top of the dresser and walked back to the bedroom door to unlock it. She began her nightly routine of getting ready for bed. In spite of her nerves being on edge, there was a rush of adrenaline that Beth felt flowing throughout her body. Her thoughts were consumed as she thought of the words that, left with no other choice, she would soon be saying to the man she had married all those years ago. For the second day in a row, Beth Jackson chose to be proactive. This time she had full intentions of only moving forward.

Chapter 11

The lights were turned off in the master bedroom as Beth lie in bed looking at the light that crept in from under the closed door. Eventually, the door swung open, and the light lit up the entire room as David was entering. Beth could only see the outline of his body. The brightness had caused her to quickly close her eyes. She opened them and squinted as they continued to adjust to the light. She then saw David very clearly with a look of surprise on his face as his hand remained on the light switch.

Seeing Beth sit up in bed with opened eyes, David asked, "Did I wake you up?"

"No" Beth replied, "I've been awake."

"Oh, good." David replied, as if he truly cared, as he turned the light switch off and continued on into the bathroom.

Beth pushed back the sheet that had covered her as she got out of bed and began walking toward the bathroom. She reached for the door handle and realized that David had locked the door. Just as she was about to knock on the door, she heard the water in the shower begin to run and the sound of music playing from the small bathroom speaker. David's late night shower playlist was something that Beth had become accustomed to hearing while in bed half asleep. Though it was a small speaker, the bathroom's acoustics projected its sound into the bedroom. It had always been a slight annoyance to Beth, but she had never said anything about it. It seemed to reach another level of irritation as she stood wide awake, right outside the bathroom door. She knew that much of it had to do with the fact that she was once again left having to play the waiting game.

She turned around with a sigh as she exhaled the deep breath that she had taken and took a seat on the edge of the bed. She looked at the yellow folder that remained on top of the dresser and felt the spark that had been lit within her slowly begin to fade. The longer Beth waited, the more reluctant she was to create change instead of continuing to wish for it. As her legs began to shake, Beth stood back up and paced back and forth as her eyes continually shifted from the envelope to the bathroom door. Hearing the shower turn off, Beth quickly grabbed the envelope from the dresser. Before she could open the dresser's bottom drawer, she heard the bathroom door lock click. Being left with no other option, she hurriedly shoved the envelope under one of her pillows. By the time the bathroom door was opened and the steam released into the bedroom, Beth had managed to make it back to her spot on the edge of the bed.

David saw her sitting there looking directly at him. "Oh, sorry. Did you need to get in? I thought you had already finished in there since you were in bed." he said, while walking into the closet.

"No." Beth started to say as the closet door shut behind him. After a couple of seconds, the door opened and David came out wearing his pajamas. Beth stood up and continued as David headed to bed, "No, I was really taking in that music you were kind enough to play."

"Yeah, I bet so." David said as he lay down and turned his lamp on.

Beth walked back over to her side of the bed and asked, "I mean, did you really think I was asleep?" as she remained standing.

"You usually are every other night." he said as he began to scroll through his phone.

"I'm sure that's what you tell yourself." Beth quietly said. "When people do inconsiderate things they tend to only believe what they choose to believe."

"Inconsiderate?" David asked as he temporarily looked up from his phone, "Beth come on, it's just music on a small speaker."

"That I can hear loud and clear when I am lying here trying to sleep. Yes!" Beth said.

"Beth, what's going on? You've had this conflicting, back and forth mood all day." David said as he shifted positions.

Beth stumbled, "I-I just. I don't-"

"I mean, where's Beth from dinner tonight?" David asked as he reached over for his phone charger. "Was that just some act to entertain the kids? I sure enjoyed it, but-"

Beth cut him off, "I just wanted their memory of the last time the four of us were together as a family to be a good one."

David quickly looked over at her with a confused expression and, after a few speechless seconds between the two of them, he cracked a smile and said, "It's been a long day, long weekend. I think you need some sleep." as he turned his nightstand lamp off.

Beth remained standing beside the bed in the pitch black as David pulled up the covers and turned his back to her while getting comfortable. She then reached under her pillow, pulled out the envelope and turned on her nightstand lamp. Without any further delay and before David could turn around to complain about the light, Beth held the envelope in front of him where the letters on it were fully visible.

"No. I think you need to wake up." Beth said in a firm voice.

It took David a few seconds to understand what exactly the envelope was about; but as he made the realization, he slowly took it from Beth's hands. With the yellow envelope now in David's possession, Beth sat down on the side of the bed as he quickly rolled over to face her. She saw the look on his face change into a smirk as he tossed the envelope over to her side of the bed. It was clear that he wanted nothing to do with it.

Beth silently shook her head as she saw his reaction and she headed head toward the door. When she got to the end of the bed, David, with a more serious facial expression, said, "Hey Beth!"

Beth stopped and turned around toward him. "Would you mind turning off your lamp?" he asked.

In complete disbelief and humiliation, Beth walked back to her side of the bed and turned off the lamp. David turned his back to her once again and laid his head on the pillow as he tried to regain comfort. In the pitch black room, Beth felt as if she had to get out of that room. She grabbed her pillow and headed for the bedroom door. As she went through the doorway, she closed the door behind her with force. The closer she got to the living room couch, the less control she had over her emotions; and by the time she flopped down on it, she began to weep with her face pressed against the leather cushion. She eventually wrapped up in the couch blanket in an attempt to get some sleep for the busy week that was ahead of her.

In the master bedroom, despite his more comfortable sleeping situation, David was not having much luck falling asleep as his thoughts were consumed with the envelope that was laying right behind him in Beth's place. He finally sat up and turned on his nightstand lamp. He looked over to her side of the bed from which she was absent for the second night in a row. Seeing the yellow envelope face up with *Stevenson Family Law* in large, bold letters, David reluctantly grabbed it and opened it. He picked a random sheet of paper out of the many that were inside and pulled it out. Before reading it, David stopped himself and shoved it back in the envelope that he then threw off of the bed. He let out a deep breath after turning his lamp off once again and lying flat on his back. David looked up to the ceiling in the complete darkness … it looked no different from the view he had when his eyes were closed.

His mind kept churning while he laid there recapping the events of the weekend. It all resembled a roller coaster. David's eyes grew heavier while he thought of the day before. Though he felt like an eternity had passed since then, there was still a fresh opportunity available that seemed to have his name sealed on it. By the time David fell asleep, his recent low moments had become an afterthought as the high points were back at the forefront of his mind.

Those high points were on his mind as he began his usual routine early the next morning. There was only one hiccup in his train of thought, and it came shortly before leaving home to begin his Monday morning. On his way to the kitchen to turn on the coffee maker, he stopped in the living room where he saw Beth lying on the couch. He stood there as she slowly breathed in and out and appeared to be peaceful … but that was far from what she was truly feeling.

David looked over to the kitchen. It was a room over in the home's open floor plan. He saw the coffee maker that was almost staring him down. He could imagine the sound it made. However, with the rare guilt he experienced, David realized that he owed it to Beth to allow her all the sleep she needed. With that thought, he decided that McDonald's coffee would do; so he gathered his things and walked out the door.

When he arrived at the local gym to work out, his mind went back to a peaceful place. This allowed his thoughts full freedom to shift back toward the good things in life. The place where he felt most at home and where he spent more time than anywhere else was categorized as one of those good things, and was also his next stop. For most people, Monday mornings are not the most welcome as families separate to go to work or school. David, however, felt the exact opposite. Clear View High School was his safe haven and the place on his mind even during the weekends at home.

Though he was now in reach of another job opportunity at an entirely different place, the school itself had become the reason behind the refreshing feeling more so than his actual job. It was the feeling he got when entering through the side locker room door. The walk to his office when passing through the locker room doors was not the most pleasant smell, but it represented tradition and many memories. It was the admiration he received from the administration, staff, and students throughout the day. That appreciation, he had recently come to understand, could have very well been associated with the fact that he was a winner. He knew the odds for winning were much lower in the near future, and that was why his next move was now his top priority. Despite that, David decided to fully soak in the feeling that came along with the attention of his admirers on a daily basis the during last couple of weeks that remained in the school year.

The end of a long school year was often viewed as a drag for both the students and the staff, but not for David. He had different feelings about the place than most within it. At this time each year, he always held on tightly to every moment and began looking forward to preparing for the next basketball season. This preparation began in the final weeks of each school year as the incoming freshman and returning players would begin after school workouts. It was always an opportunity to get a glimpse of what the next year would look like. It was the time when he could see what he would have to work with … which in prior years had been great talent. There had always been talk of the next star player either about to enter high school or one who showed a lot of promise on the JV team. In recent years however, there had been fewer and fewer with that kind of talent, and David had relied heavily on his upperclassmen players. Now that they were graduating, the future of Clear View High's basketball team was in question.

Future success here was something David knew was highly unlikely, and he felt relief as he thought about not being there to experience defeat. He looked at the name list for the first workout scheduled for the next day. The list of names seemed to get shorter each year, and the talent was on a steady decline. He thought back to his first years as a coach and when the current seniors were on the list. For incoming freshmen, there had been long notes from the Clear View Middle School coach beside each name that accurately described their talent and potential. The only notes that appeared as David looked at the current list were comments such as, "He is barely academically eligible. Keep an eye on his grades." or "Better kid than athlete, but is a good teammate." David was not sure which note was more useless and had no interest in seeing any of them. Thinking of it, he felt sorry for the individual who would potentially take his place. David put the paper down and wondered who might be in the running to take his place. When he looked straight ahead and saw Marshal Lee's desk, his eyes widened.

"*Marshal*" David said quietly.

Not only would Marshal most likely be the first choice to take over as head coach, he still had not been made aware of David's interview at ESU. David knew that had to change. When Marshal Lee did eventually make his way through the Coach's office door at his usual time, David was waiting for him. With only a few minutes before the school bell rang, he needed to break the news quickly. David realized just how difficult doing that would be.

Looking as upbeat as ever, he said to David, "Morning, Coach."

"There he is. Good Morning." replied David. "Good weekend?"

"Ah, you know." Marshal said as he smiled and sat his bag down on the desk. "The usual."

"Oh yeah, *the usual*." David said with a laugh.

"Hey, I needed a good time before seeing these knuckleheads that we have to work with next year. Did you see that list that was emailed to us? Pitiful!" Marshal said.

"Yeah." David said as he held up the paper, "I have it printed."

"Mmhh, anyway … what about your weekend?" Marshal asked.

"Well." David said, "There wasn't much usual about mine."

"Is that a good thing or bad?" asked Marshal.

"Really good! and bad. Well … more difficult than bad, I guess."

"Man, I can't tell you how many weekends have ended up that way for me. It'll be really good at night, then the sun comes up the next morning and I'm questioning life itself, and then-" Marshal said.

"No, no." David said, stopping Marshal, seeing where he was going with his story. "That's not exactly my situation" David continued, "Well I guess it's *our* situation now."

"What do you mean?" asked Marshal as he took a seat at his desk.

David knew he could no longer hold off on what needed to be said to him. He cut right to the chase by telling Marshal, "I interviewed for the head coaching position at ESU on Saturday. There's no guarantee, but it went really well."

Marshal's facial expression suddenly turned serious, as did his tone, "Oh … *oh*. *Our* situation, I see."

"Yeah." said David as he propped his elbows on his desk.

"ESU, huh?" Marshal said.

"Yeah" David replied, feeling as if that was all he knew to say.

"That's big time, man." said Marshal, "I mean … that's all you. If it works out, you wouldn't have to worry about your big legacy around here. That's what you wanted right?"

Unsure if Marshal was sincere, David replied, "Uh … yeah. That's true I guess."

The school bell interrupted their conversation as it rang loudly through the school's intercom speakers. Marshal stood up from his chair and said, "I think there's a gym full of high schoolers for us to tend to."

As Marshal left the office, David remained seated at his desk. He could clearly see the way his assistant coach felt about the news that he had just been told. The obvious shift from Marshal's outgoing mood was a tough thing for David to observe. There had always been nothing but respect between the two men. Marshal had always looked up to David as a coach and learned a lot just by watching him interact with the team and all of the students at Clear View. Despite their age difference, they were also able to connect on a personal level as their personalities meshed well together. Aside from the talent they coached, it was their working relationship that determined the overall success of the team. David appreciated how important their relationship was and spent the entire day trying to salvage it.

David repeatedly assured Marshal that he would be present at the next day's workouts and that he was committed to his team and to his job until the very end. Deep down, there was an entirely different feeling. It was a clear contrast to his promise. The only commitment he was willing to offer was to his friend and fellow coach, Marshal. David's heart was no longer in the job that had seemingly led him to a dead end after the long road of success. Though Marshal had told David that he was fine with the possibility of him leaving, David found that hard to believe. It led him to attempt explaining himself in more depth when the two were alone in the office during their planning period.

While the two pretended to be occupied on their laptops in the quiet room, David finally closed his screen and said, "I wouldn't have taken that interview if I didn't believe that this team would be in good hands."

Marshal looked up from his screen with a facial expression that clearly showed his disbelief.

"I'm not so sure about that." said Marshal.

"What do you mean?" asked David.

"You're telling me that the one thing on your mind when you agreed to that interview was that the team was in good hands?" Marshal asked him.

"Well, yeah." David replied, not sounding so sure of himself.

Marshal chuckled while shaking his head and said, "Whatever you say, Coach." and looked back to his laptop.

It was obvious that the two men still were not on the same page, but David would soon see that he had spent his time trying to salvage the wrong relationship in his life.

Chapter 12

David drove home from work earlier than usual that afternoon. Near the end of his short drive from the school and only a half mile from his neighborhood, he noticed a truck that he recognized very well. It was very distinguishable with its large bed that was so wide it could be seen from the front of the truck. It was also the brightest shade of red that there could possibly be on a vehicle. As David passed it, he could see through the windshield the white haired man driving it. That was official proof of what he had already known about the truck and its owner. The man driving it was the one he had always known as "Mr. Taylor" ... or more importantly as his father-in-law.

As David turned into the neighborhood he wondered what Mr. Taylor would have been doing on this side of town. It was Mrs. Taylor who would often pick up the kids from school and take them home with her for Beth to pick up. He then thought perhaps Mr. Taylor had been substituted for pick up duty, which would have been one of the few reasons that he would possibly leave home. Ever since his retirement, Mr. Taylor would only make it as far as his home workshop, church, and the occasional grocery run. Even David knew this information, though it had been quite some time since he had seen his father-in-law. These were just well-known facts about the man.

As he thought more about it, David knew Beth would still be at work at this time of the day and there was no one at home to watch the kids. David then thought, *Great, he's dropped off the kids to be home by themselves ... smart.*

When he finally turned into his driveway, David got out of his truck, rushed up the steps, and unlocked the door. As soon as the front door opened, the reason for Mr. Taylor's visit to this side of town was very clear. He had come to drop off something entirely different than what David had assumed. In front of David were several rows of cardboard moving boxes that were nearly as tall as he was. Beside them was a stack of boxes that had yet to be assembled; and on top of the stack was a piece of paper. David bent down, picked up the paper and read the words on it, *"Beth, I hope these boxes work for you. Let me know if you need anymore. I will come back with my truck to help get your items moved to our house. The key is back under the mat on the front porch. Love you, always. See you soon. Dad"*

David placed the paper back on the unassembled boxes and took a few steps back. The sight awakened him to the tough truth of the matter. The delusions and theories that he had built in his mind about his marriage were about to crash down and quickly fade away. Standing there feeling almost numb, David felt as if the walls around him were beginning to close in. He knew he had to get out of there or he would experience a soul-crushing suffocation. What he was not so sure of was where he would go, but such a thing was not important to him at that moment. He could just no longer stand to see the sight of the ultimate result of his wrongdoings. Then he thought about the kids ... wondering if Elijah and Molly really had in fact been dropped off in addition to the boxes.

"Kids?!" He yelled with a loud voice.

David ran up the stairs and peaked into each of the kid's rooms to make sure that they were not home. After seeing two empty bedrooms, he rushed back downstairs and approached the front door. He absentmindedly opened it and was halfway out before coming to a stop. David turned around and took another look at the stack of boxes. At that moment he knew exactly where he would go. He murmured to himself, "I guess two of us can play this 'packing' game." He had his office at Clear View High in mind. With the hope and strong belief that he had about the new job and his chances of obtaining it, David thought that he too would need to do some packing, and he might as well get a head start in doing so. It was the perfect escape and the most reasonable thought that came to him. He walked toward the tall stack of boxes and grabbed one from the top. With it in hand, David walked out of the door and headed straight for his refuge.

The parking lot of Clear View High was half empty when David arrived. He parked near the locker room hall entrance door and went in with the box in hand. He gave a nod to one of the long-time school janitors who was vacuuming in the hallway. He unlocked the office door, flipped up the light switch, and walked over to his desk that was layered with papers. It was then that he realized what he was getting himself into. He opened a desk drawer to see that it was nearly full and realized that a trash bag would suit him better than a box. However, there were so many keepsakes around the desk. Various coaching award certificates and many newspaper clippings from the local paper were pinned on a bulletin board. Some of them dated back to his playing days. The most treasured item from his desk area was the collection of pictures of his past teams and former players in their college jerseys.

There was nothing that made David prouder as a coach than those things. Though they were in his daily work space, he hardly ever took the time to look back and reminisce. It wasn't that he preferred not to, but the future just always had its grip on David. It consumed his thoughts and actions and was exactly why he was in his office with a moving box at that point in the day. However, his pathway to future endeavors always led to a pause for appreciation of the past ones, which turned out to be something he did not mind. The moments in front of the Clear View trophy case and the ESU athletic office lobby was a brief time of reflection that provided an escape from the current circumstances of his life. Reading a few of the articles and flipping through old photos did the same thing for David, but he realized it was time to press play once again.

David went through each desk drawer thinking to toss away the meaningless items in them. However, he quickly realized that there were even more keepsakes, including old letters from players and other small mementos that had been placed in the drawers and forgotten. Coming across those things slowed the packing process, but it was exactly what David needed. He began to think that an even bigger box was necessary as the trash pile was much smaller than he had anticipated. He finished going through the three left drawers, and the job was halfway complete. Before starting on the three to his right, he stood up from his chair to see if there may be more boxes anywhere around. As he walked to the storage closet in the back of the office, he heard his cell phone begin to ring.

David immediately reached inside his pocket for the phone, where it would usually be, before hearing it vibrate against a hard surface. He turned and saw the phone lying flat on his desk and rushed to it, picking it up and turning it over to see the name "Daniel Simmons" on the screen. He had been so preoccupied with the events of the day that he had paid little attention to his phone. He had been distracted to the point of forgetting that a call about the job was expected. Seeing Daniel's name was like ice cold water waking him up and bringing him to his senses. After the phone rang one more time, David quickly swiped his finger across the screen to answer the call.

"Daniel! How's it going?" he said.

"Good. I see your name was on Mr. Cunningham's call list for today. Have you heard anything from him?" Daniel asked.

David replied while looking at the time on his watch, "Well … no. I haven't heard anything yet. I don't think he's called. It's been a crazy day but I'm pretty sure … no, I haven't heard anything."

Daniel responded, "Okay. Just make sure you're on standby for the call. It should be coming at any minute now. So I'll hang up and talk to you later, alright?"

"Yeah … yeah okay, that sounds good." David replied as he hung up the phone.

As soon as the call ended, David checked his recent call list to make sure that he had not missed a call. He was relieved, but he grew even more anxious when he saw that he had received no calls during the day. His mind went back into its usual fast forward mode, but his hand was glued to the cell phone, gripping it tightly in anticipation. He leaned back in his chair and looked straight ahead. The thoughts inside his head were solely on the expected call. He reached for the top drawer to his right to continue the packing, but he could not go any further than grabbing the handle. The idea of doing anything else other than waiting for the call was simply impossible.

David rocked the office chair back and forth while staring up at the clock on the opposite wall. He continuously looked down at his phone to make sure it was not on silent and that the volume was turned all the way up. Though it was later into the afternoon, he knew that a call from Mr. Cunningham was possible at any time of the day. David had seen first-hand during the interview how spastic Mr. Cunningham's schedule could become. He took a deep breath and leaned even further back in his chair as his eyelids began to get heavy. They eventually closed shut while the cell phone remained in his hand, David was certain a short nap would not harm anything.

Only a few minutes into his relaxing, the loud sound of a phone ringing caused him to jump up. With his widened eyes, he looked down at his cell phone only to see a black screen. As another ring came, he quickly realized it was the office phone on his desk. He let out an annoyed and disappointed sigh while he placed his cell phone on the desk.

He picked up the office phone and let out a less than enthusiastic, "Yes?"

"Oh, hey!" the lady's voice said on the other line, "I had a good feeling that you'd still be working."

David recognized the upbeat voice immediately as the school's front desk worker.

"Yes." he replied, "I'm *still* here."

"A parent called and had a question about tomorrow's basketball workouts. What time do they end?" the lady asked.

Just as she finished asking the question, David heard his cell phone start vibrating on the desk as it began to ring its familiar tone. With the office phone in one hand, David looked at his screen to see a number he did not recognize. *It has to be Mr. Cunningham*, he thought.

David quickly replied to the front desk worker, "They end at four thirty."

"Four thirty. Okay." she replied, "And there might have been one other thing."

David's leg began to shake while he glanced back at his cell phone as it continued to ring.

"Nope." she continued, "I think that's it. Have a good-"

"Great. Bye." David said, cutting her off while slamming the office phone down into its cradle at the same time.

He picked up his cell phone and was able to answer it just before it finished ringing.

"This is David Jackson."

"David, this is Ben Cunningham here. It's good to hear your voice again. I apologize for calling so late in the day, but I wanted to go ahead and reach out to you before tomorrow."

Just relieved about receiving the call, David replied, "Oh, it's no problem."

"Well, look it was really great talking to you the other day. I thoroughly enjoyed it." Mr. Cunningham replied.

"Likewise." David replied as he remembered the long, drawn out conversation they shared. "I enjoyed the *interview*." he continued, trying to put emphasis on the purpose of their talk.

"Yes, a good conversation." Mr. Cunningham said. "I've had the privilege of talking to many great candidates for our open head coaching position. It's been quite a hectic time trying to fill it. But there were no other candidates like you."

"Oh, well that's interesting to hear." David replied, unsure of what that meant.

"You were the only one on the list who was not a college coach. As I said before, you're a winner, and we do need a winner's mindset in our basketball program."

Liking where Mr. Cunningham was going, David leaned back in his chair and coolly said, "I totally agree."

"In order to get that winner's mindset, I firmly believe that experience is needed to build a foundation to do so." After a short pause Mr. Cunningham said, "And to be honest, I'd feel really guilty throwing you into that situation."

"Oh?" said David as he slowly leaned up from his seat.

"David, you've got a good thing going over there at Clear View. I don't want to take that away from you all of a sudden." said Mr. Cunningham in a soft tone.

Losing his patience, David replied, "Sir, cut the crap."

"We're going in a different direction. We're hiring a long-time coach who's coming out of retirement to help rebuild the program."

David was silent and he could feel the palm of his right hand that held the cell phone against his ear began to sweat.

Hearing no response on the other end of the line and sensing David's disappointment, Ben Cunningham continued, "I know you have a bright future, David, and one day I believe you'll bring your success as a coach to the college level. Now is just not the time."

David heard the compliments but they went in one ear and quickly out the other. He did not have a single ounce of belief in what Mr. Cunningham had just said. The latter part would be all that he remembered. Everything else that Ben Cunningham had told him was useless to David. *"Now is just not the time"* is what echoed in David's head as his silence continued. It was all he could do to stop himself from hanging up without showing a small sign of decency.

"Thank you for reaching out to me." he said in an attempt to hide his dismay.

"No ... thank you, David. You're a heck of a guy."

In one ear and out the other.

David began to lower the phone from his ear before Ben continued by saying, "Matter of fact ..."

David quickly put his cell phone back against his ear and listened intently for any other form of opportunity offered that would allow him to go elsewhere. Assistant coach, team manager, ball boy, water boy, he would take any of it.

"Anytime you need another good talk, I have some extra season tickets. I'd love to share them with you and watch a game sometime just let me know when you're-"

Wanting nothing to do with an offer that had no worth to him, David had listened to all he could take, and he hung up the phone before Ben finished. Sitting completely still, consumed with the feeling of dejection, he stared straight ahead with a blank look on his face. He not only began to slowly loosen his grip on the cell phone, but more importantly on the belief he had held so strongly. It was his optimism that had finally let him down; and for the first time, David's charisma was not strong enough to get him where he wanted to be. From the first moment he was made aware of the job, it was far from a want. David had desperately felt that he *needed* it. The job opportunity had become a crutch on which to lean the weight of his heavy personal burdens. Now that it had finally snapped, David was left with no other option but to fall deeper into the dark caverns of emotion that he had never experienced. He sat there feeling like a small speck in a huge world that he once felt he had complete control over. The day's prior event had already left him feeling small, but he had now been downsized to an unimaginable level.

David tossed the cell phone that he had held tightly in his right hand onto his desk and put his hands on the arms of his office chair. When he threw his head back against the chair, he placed his hands over his eyes; and they eventually worked their way through his hair. When David placed them back on the arm of his chair, he looked at the packing box directly in front of him. It was nearly full. He then rolled the chair back enough to bring his legs from under the desk onto the top of it. With both feet crossed on top of the desk, they were right against the box. The blank expression on his face turned into one that screamed rage. That feeling began to work its way through his body.

David brought his right leg back and forcefully kicked the packing box off the desk and onto the floor. As the papers and pictures spilled out of the box, he cocked his right leg back even further and kicked the long metal drawer in the middle of his desk as hard as he could. He then quickly stood up from his seat, placed both hands under the dented drawer, and started to lift up on the desk. With the right side of the desk being much heavier than the left, David's attention was diverted allowing him to stop himself from causing any more damage to the desk or himself. However, it was himself that he saw in the desk, which is where his anger was directed. David pictured the many drawers that he had closed shut in his life where the memorable, lasting things were locked away and forgotten. There had always been a fear of opening them up. He was afraid of the regret he would feel from the moments that were left behind in pursuit of his own dreams and desires. In one single moment, every drawer had been opened and everything within them was exposed.

Chapter 13

David Jackson stood still in front of the office chair and observed the mess that he had made. Breathing heavily and on the verge of tears, suddenly a smile came across his face as he looked at the sight before him. With both hands on his hips, seeing the dented desk and the scattered papers that were of his doing led David to chuckle. *What are the odds?* he thought to himself. Finding his tough luck hysterical had caused a full range of emotions to pass through his system. David leaned forward and slammed both hands flat on the desk. With his head faced downward, the laughing continued to build. He then reached his right hand forward and placed it on his cell phone. Touching it lightly, he slowly slid the cell phone toward himself as it remained screen down on the desk.

He was quiet as he lifted his head and turned the phone over to see the time on the screen display. David put the phone in his pocket and checked his other one to feel for his truck keys. He decided that it was time to head elsewhere. Before leaving the office, he paused at the door to take another look around his desk area. This time he found nothing funny about it. Instead he let out a somber sigh, flipped down the light switch, and headed out. After locking the door behind him, David walked down the hallway that was now dark. He headed toward the end of the hallway where the glass door let in light from the outside. Before pushing it open, David stopped for a moment and turned toward the locker room hallway that led to his office. In only a matter of seconds, he sensed the strong odor; and the very thought of walking through it at the beginning and end of every workday gave him a feeling of discouragement. In times past, David had become nose blind to the smell that had represented good memories and great traditions. However, at this moment, the odor felt sickening as he thought about his unstable future as a coach there. He felt the same dread he had before being aware of the ESU coaching opportunity.

David opened the door and walked to his truck that was parked near the building. He realized he had no place to go at that moment other than back to his personal life at home. It had become an equal contributor to his dread of the future; and after seeing all the packing boxes there, he knew more uncertainty was imminent. As he unlocked his truck door, he wondered what he would find when he got home. That thought began to overtake his emotions. He had always kept the two main factions of his life separate, but now they had begun to overlap. David was no longer able to fall back on either one. He felt as if both hands were tied and he was completely outmatched. He opened the truck door and got inside.

Still feeling overcome by the events of the day, David sat in the driver's seat and just stared out into the darkening space in front of him. As he sat there, he surrendered to the heart-wrenching feeling that was growing inside his chest. He reached in his pocket and pulled out the keys only to toss them onto the passenger seat. He forcefully placed both hands on the steering wheel and held onto it with a tight grip. As if he was trying to rip the steering wheel out, David's arms began to shake it back and forth. A sense of numbness came over him to the extent that he could see the steering wheel but could not feel it. He could hear the loud scream that he let out, but could not feel his burning throat vibrations. As he jammed down on the horn, it's output simply blended in among the many other noises that were defeating any sense of sanity he had left.

What David did not see was a man who was walking almost directly in front of his truck during his breakdown. The man was startled when he heard the horn loud and clear. Stopping directly in front of the truck, he thought he had seen it before. Taking a closer look, he could see David through the windshield and was then able to identify the truck for sure. The man walked to the driver's side door and knocked on the window. David's eyes were closed; and his mind was in such a state at that point he didn't hear the man knocking. It was not until the man began to yell from outside the truck that David became aware of his presence. His eyes quickly opened and a feeling of embarrassment swept over him. He pressed the window switch on his door, but the window would not go down. David continued to poke at the button as his embarrassment grew. Then he realized he had never put the key in the ignition. He opened his door to get out. Upon seeing such a distraught person opening the truck door, the man took a few steps backward.

As David got out, he said, "How's it going?"

"Coach Jackson? I thought that was you." the man said.

"Guilty." said David, who tried to think of where he had seen this man before.

"Winning rubs off quick, doesn't it?" said the man.

"You could say that, yeah." David replied.

"You always seem to be the last man in every parking lot around here."

"I usually work pretty late." said David.

"Work pretty late, arrive pretty late. Same difference." the man said.

Seeing David's puzzled look, the man continued, "I saw you at the middle school a while back. I think I caught you at a rough time then, too. I'm guessing you had just missed your boy's play?"

David had made so many missteps that they were hard to keep track of, but he was able to remember that moment … and the man who reminded him of it.

"What are you doing here?" asked David, who associated him as working at his son's school.

"I come here and help do some extra cleaning after I finish at the middle school." the man replied.

"I see. Well, I don't want to keep you from your work any longer." David replied as he began to make his way back in the truck.

The man nodded as David got back in his truck. He stood there in place and watched as David drove away. He remained in place until David's truck was out of sight. Then walking toward the school building, the man could not help but feel glad that he was not in Coach Jackson's shoes. Though his own life was grueling on a daily basis, and despite the fact that he was about to spend even more time cleaning up after other people, the man had never once been close to feeling the intense frustration he had just witnessed.

While David made the short drive back home, "intense" did not do justice in describing his true feelings. The combination of the many mixed emotions that had blended inside him to cause his extreme explosion seemed to be brewing again. He decided that the best thing for him was to be alone. He knew that the last scenario he wanted to deal with was to arrive home and find Beth and the kids, along with his in-laws, carrying Beth's boxes out of his house. David understood that the rage he had unleashed was intoxicating and that he had little control over his emotions. He was already embarrassed enough that someone he did not even know saw it. He did not want to even imagine his own kids observing such a thing.

Upon arriving home, David felt he had a small break. Nobody was there, nor would he expect anyone to be for the rest of the evening. When he walked through the front door, he saw that the tall stack of boxes was no longer there. Glancing around the room, he found that most everything else remained intact. The half-empty house he had imagined Beth would leave him was not the case. Everything, even the photos and other decorations that Beth had set up, were all in place. It was not until he walked into the master bedroom closet that he missed something. He saw there that her entire side of the closet was nearly empty. The sight was still not enough to derail him, but he did not have the courage to go upstairs. He was afraid that he would see the same thing in the bedrooms of Elijah and Molly. Feeling as if that would put him over the edge, David remained downstairs and tried to make it a normal evening.

The next morning was a different story as David made no attempt to seek normalcy. It began when his phone alarm sounded. He did not budge. When the sound became such an annoyance he could no longer endure it, he finally reached his left arm out to the nightstand for his phone. After pressing the snooze button, he rolled over feeling no desire to start his day. After several more minutes, the alarm sounded again. David finally made the full effort to sit up and unplug his phone from the charger. Going to the gym was out of the question now; but after seeing the time on the screen, he saw there was plenty of time to spare before he had to be at work. With that thought, he tossed his phone aside, laid back down and shut his eyes once again.

It was not long before a restless feeling began to stir in him. This led him to get out of bed and head to the kitchen to make his morning cup of coffee. After a few sips, he thought to himself that that no amount of caffeine could create the enthusiasm that was missing in every aspect of his life. With the coffee mug sitting to his right and a spoon full of yogurt in his left hand, David sat at the quiet kitchen table alone. He still did not have any idea as to just how different the home's atmosphere would be that particular morning. He had always steered clear from the hectic weekday mornings in his household and did not have the slightest clue about the chaos that Beth had been left to handle on her own. His normal daily routine was always a grab-and-go breakfast that he never ate until he arrived at school after his workout and shower.

As he pulled out his phone he was tempted to call the school and let them know he was taking a sick day. He got as far as going to his contact list. He scrolled down as far as the "C's" where he noticed "Coach Marshall Lee" before finding "Clear View High," which was just above Coach Lee's name on the list. Seeing the name of his loyal co-worker and friend caused David to gain a sense of motivation that motivated him to get up from the kitchen table, get himself ready, and begin his Tuesday morning. He could not let Marshal down and leave him in the dust on what was to be an important day for the basketball program's uncertain future. Though David was taking the steps to start his day, the outlook on his circumstances had not changed in any way. This reigned true as he turned into the Clear View High School parking lot and an uneasy feeling of angst came over him. As David navigated his way around to his usual parking space, he noticed that Marshal Lee's car was already there in the next space over. Knowing Marshal's usual arrival time, David looked at his watch and saw that he was later than he thought. Though David was later than usual, there was still half an hour before the school day began, and it was Marshal who had arrived early.

David approached the building at a quick pace and entered through the locker room hallway's side door. He jogged toward the coach's office and then slowed down to gain his composure before entering.

"Well, well, well." Marshal said while turning his chair around as David walked in. "I finally beat you to it."

"Sorry about that." David replied as he approached his desk.

"I'm guessing you have the whole 'two-week notice, senioritis' vibe going on now." said Marshal.

"I'm a little late, but cut me some slack. You're here earlier than usual." David said.

"Well, I got to thinking after yesterday." Marshal began. "I thought about the possibility of you not being around here next year, and I realized that I needed to take more responsibility."

"I see. That's a good idea." David said, feeling more impressed than he sounded.

"Now, I'm not trying to call myself the new head coach or anything; and don't worry, I didn't go around spreading the news about your interview either." Marshal assured David.

David, feeling unprepared to share the truth about his future plans, replied, "Well, that's a good thing. Thank you for that."

"No worries. So I decided to start planning drills for the guys to do at the workout this afternoon. Feel free to take a look, and let me know what you think." said Marshal.

"Oh yeah, I'll do that. Just let me get settled in first." David said as he rummaged through his bag, which he had put on the desk.

Marshal turned back to his laptop keyboard and began typing. While looking at his screen, he said to David, "I also see that moving box on your desk. You're always thinking ahead."

Yesterday's late afternoon visit to the office was the last thing David wanted to think about. He looked down at his middle desk drawer that was dented and remembered the anger he had demonstrated and the mess he had left as a result of it.

"Ha, yeah. So was this box on my desk when you walked in today?" David asked, wondering if Marshal had cleaned up the papers that he had left scattered on the floor that were now back inside of the moving box.

"What do you mean?" asked Marshal.

"Like … was the box sitting here or was it somewhere else?" David asked.

Marshal replied, "No, I didn't move it. It was right there where it is now when I came in." He continued, "Don't you worry, I didn't go digging through your stuff."

David pushed the box aside and found a note that had been placed beside it. It read, "*Coach Jackson, I found these items on the floor while vacuuming. Based on what I just saw in the parking lot, I thought this was of your doing and figured they belonged in the box. I hope to catch you in a better place the next time we cross paths. Don't let the wins rub off too quickly.*"

David now had absolutely no question as to who had written the note. He easily traced it back to the man he had encountered during two personal and professional low points. Sitting down in his chair, he looked back down at the note again and repeatedly read the last sentence several times. "*Don't let the wins rub off too quickly.*"

Reading the note caused David to think about what he should consider a win. For all these years it had all been about winning as a coach … sports … his teams … his pride. But in this moment of reflection, he began to think about things that did not include a trophy or any form of praise. The small victories that could have made all the difference in his life are what came to mind as David began to reexamine wins that had nothing to do with basketball. He realized the simple task of getting out of bed that morning could count as a win. The fact that he was sitting in the exact same spot where his dreams had been crushed should not be taken lightly. David understood it showed a sign of courage to continue pushing forward even as it seemed that there was nothing on the horizon for him that was worth his effort.

He folded the note and placed it inside of the moving box with the many other items that David would keep and appreciate. After moving the box to the floor beside his desk, he began to clear space for his laptop. He was ready to begin his day and ultimately preparation for the inevitable future season that was ahead at Clear View.

David opened his laptop and asked Marshal, "Would you mind emailing me the list of drills you were working on for the workouts? I'd be happy to review them."

"Sure thing, Coach." Marshal replied.

From the moment the school day began and until the last bell rang, it was that short note that boosted David's thoughts to make it through in high spirits. It was very rare for David's sights to be set on the present … not on the future nor the past, but the present. He still was not ready to tell Marshal he did not get the job, so he shied away from thinking of it. He feared it may destroy his current outlook and that outlook was critical in his surviving the day. David's focus on finding any form of victory in his life had also led him to avoid two calls and a text message from Daniel Simmons. Daniel knew about the direction ESU was taking, and David was not ready to revisit his own road of loss just yet. He would revisit it at a later time with Daniel.

Making it to the end of the school day was only the beginning. The basketball workouts began shortly after the dismissal bell rang, and the players headed straight to the locker rooms to change. The rising freshmen coming from Clear View Middle School always arrived at the first workouts by bus and were already on their way as their school day ended fifteen minutes before the high school. Their coach usually drove the bus and stayed to help David and Marshal with the workouts. While the players changed, David stood by the door in the locker room hallway to let the middle school players in and welcome them along with their coach. While looking through the glass door, he saw a minivan pull into the parking lot. David thought nothing of it until the van parked right by the door. It was then that he recognized the man driving as the middle school coach.

David thought, *What the-* but then opened the door and put on a smile.

"Afternoon, Coach Jackson." the middle school coach said as he walked around the van and opened the sliding door for his players to get out.

"Hey there, Coach G." David said, trying his best to sound enthusiastic.

As a few of the players began to exit the minivan, it became clear to David why it served as their transportation instead of a bus. He nodded as each one entered through the door that he held open. He was not at all impressed by his first look at the young men. David could only hope another van was on its way with more players.

As Coach G closed the van door, he asked David, "Is it okay if I stay parked here?"

"That'll be fine. Since it's a minivan, I don't think it will be in anyone's way." David replied.

"Yeah, as you can tell we had fewer players sign up to come than usual, so the school wouldn't allow us to take a bus. Luckily my wife let me borrow her van." Coach G said.

As they walked down the locker room hall toward the gym, David took a deep breath and thought to himself, *here we go.*

Once all the players were dressed, everyone met at half court. It allowed David and Marshal time to do a brief introduction and to talk about the main purpose of the workouts ... *"to get better."* After explaining this, the players formed two lines for layups and rebounding to get warmed up. Soon after the players began, it was clear that a lot of work had to be done; and the main purpose of the workouts was something that drastically needed to happen.

Marshal stood beside David as they watched the players miss layups and goof off in the lines. They showed no form of structure or care to learn. Aside from that, there was little overall skill available; and it seemed like there was no desire from any of the players to gain it. Marshal looked over at David to see a cringed look of pain and disappointment on his face as he gazed ahead.

Marshal faced forward again with his arms crossed. After a few seconds more had passed and without looking in his direction, he said to David, "You didn't get the job, did you?" David continued observing the players and took a moment before responding. "How did you know?" he asked Marshal as he continued his straight gaze ahead.

Marshal said, "The look on your face is the look of a man who has no other choice but to coach these guys."

All David could do was shamefully nod his head as his mind took a sharp mental turn back toward the road of loss on which he was now forced to continue traveling. What he did not know was that a sign of hope was about to appear. As David and Marshal continued watching the players warm up, they heard the sound of the gym doors bursting open. The sound could be heard from the other side of the gym. Both coaches simultaneously looked in that direction to see a tall kid who had to duck his head slightly to get through the door. While he began jogging onto the court, David took a good look at him. He knew that he had never seen the young man before; and judging by his youthful face, he assumed he was an incoming freshman. Everything else about him though was far from immature. The way he was built, he could have passed for some of the players that David had already coached and sent off to play college basketball.

For most kids, the taller they were the lankier they would be. This kid was nearly the height of the tallest player David had ever coached. His braided hair touched the top of the gym doorway. He was carrying his basketball shoes in one hand. Both David and Marshal looked at his well-defined arms and saw nothing lanky about him. The boy took a seat on the first row of bleachers and exchanged his slide-on sandals for basketball shoes.

When he leaned forward and reached down to begin tying his shoes, Marshal gave David an elbow nudge and quietly asked, "You seeing what I'm seeing?"

"If you're seeing a sign of light in a dark tunnel … then yes!" David replied while sporting a big grin on his face.

As the boy stood up and made his way onto the court to join in one of the layup lines, David and Marshal walked over to Coach G who was observing the warmups from half court. The two men stood beside Coach G thinking that he would mention something about the young man who had just walked in.

Coach G looked at them apologetically and said, "They're really looking sloppy." while shaking his head.

"Yeah-yeah, but Coach, who's that fella right there." David asked while pointing toward the young man who had nudged his way to the front of the line and already had a ball in hand.

"Oh." Coach G replied with the same tone as he had in his description of the warm ups, "That's Sam Moore."

"*Sam Moore?*" David asked himself aloud. "I don't think I saw his name on that list you sent us."

It was Sam's turn to do a layup. He took two big dribbles from the line, palmed the basketball with his right hand, jumped up, and dunked it with force. All the boys who were supposed to be trying to get the rebound just watched in amazement before trying to retrieve the ball.

After the sound of the rim echoed loudly in the gym, Sam made his way to the back of the rebound line. Coach G spoke to him, "Take it easy, Sam. We're just warming up right now."

Sam looked at Coach G straight faced, turned his back to him, and again faced the basketball goal.

David asked Coach G, "Why haven't I heard about this kid?"

Coach G continued observing the players warming up and responded, "I'm actually glad you haven't. There's a lot of bad things to know about when it comes to him. They outnumber the good by a long shot."

"There wasn't anything bad about what I just saw. I don't know about you guys." said Marshal.

"Sam's the best athlete you'll ever see … he sure is the best one I've seen at his age. When there's a ball in his hand, it's hard to see past the good. When you've experienced him outside of sports, well … it's just bad." said Coach G while shaking his head.

"*Bad* is a pretty strong word when used to describe someone, don't you think?" asked David.

"Bad really doesn't do it justice." Coach G said. "The kid's a mess. Regardless of the sport, Sam's never been able to last a whole season without getting kicked off the team."

That was not really welcome news; but, while David watched Sam as he jumped high to grab a rebound, he couldn't help but wonder **why?**

Chapter 14

Four days later

Sam Moore woke up on Saturday morning knowing that his grandmother would be working her usual shift as an at-home nurse. Her shift lasted most of the day. This meant yet another long period of time that he would be on his own. It was her house that Sam called home and had been for most of his life. Having a father that he never met and a mother he only knew from old photographs that were beyond his memory, "home" was a complicated concept for him to grasp. He only knew it as a place that kept him cool in the summer, warm in the winter and dry from the rain. A place filled with love? Not so much! To Sam, the rare moments he and his grandmother were there at the same time felt lonelier than when she was away. Little did he know how hard it was for her, as he got older, to see past his resemblance to family who had caused her so much pain.

Still, she took responsibility for the young boy who needed a home, realizing that there was not nearly enough that she could do to fix something much deeper in him. As time went by, Sam's grandmother understood it was not only looks that had been passed down through generations, but also the same demons that haunted her own children and the man she had once loved. They could spread anger like a wildfire within the soul, and that had only led them to a road of self-destruction. She had seen the signs in Sam as it progressively grew more serious. Sam had no idea of his family's past and did not really care about it. What he did know was that there was something about himself that he had little control over. Whatever it was had gotten him into situations of which he really did not want any part, but he could not seem to stop it from happening. It always left him feeling like the odd man out and wondering "*Why me?*" which was a question his ego never allowed him to ask anyone other than himself.

Sam believed that he had done well at hiding his dark problems from his grandmother. The two of them had grown accustomed to an occasional teacher phone call about his behavior and a report card that was not impressive. Both of those matters had once been handled with a brief conversation and reprimand from his grandmother. Now she rarely mentioned his misbehavior anymore. His actions were simply ignored and forgotten until the next occurrence. Sam's grandmother knew more than he did about the problems he faced and from where they stemmed. She saw past his attempts to hide his actions. She often noticed his bloody knuckles as well as the scrapes and scars on his wrists.

Sam always got home just before time for dinner in the evenings. He told his grandmother that he spent his afternoons at the neighborhood park playing basketball. In part, that was true. When his presence was no longer welcomed on a school sports team, he had nothing else to do during his afternoons after school. He did almost always start out at the park and would stay there until his presence was not welcome there either.

The same thing happened on Saturday morning, when he woke up late in an empty house, he found a basketball and headed for the courts. As he approached the park, the usual crowd was already playing on the courts. They gathered there every day, rain or shine. "*Here he comes*" they all thought as Sam walked toward them. One boy gladly volunteered to leave the game in order for Sam to take his spot. The game continued as Sam took over, using his skill to outmatch anyone who made any attempt to guard him. He soon noticed that very little attempt was being made by those on the other team. It became obvious that everyone was just getting out of his way. When dribbling hard toward the basketball goal, Sam suddenly stopped in his tracks and held the ball.

Turning around to face them, he asked, "What's this? You guys scared or something?"

None of the other boys who were playing responded. Some of them separated themselves even further. In response to this, Sam dropped the ball and quickly approached the boy who had been half-heartedly guarding him. Sam grabbed him by the shirt and held onto it with a grip that began to stretch the front neckline.

"Did I stutter?" Sam yelled in the boy's face while towering over him.

"N-No. Man, come on." said the boy while trying to break loose.

What Sam did not see was the group of guys ganging up behind him during his rant. However, he suddenly felt two of the boys grabbing his broad shoulders and attempting to throw him to the ground. When their attempt did not work, the other boys who were standing around quickly came to assist in taking Sam down. It took every one of them to do it. They were all equally fed up with Sam's intimidation. They had reached their breaking point and decided that together they had to take action against him. Everyone began to throw punches and even kicks to keep Sam down on the ground. When he finally let up and realized that he had been outmatched, the group of boys had time to run away. Sam suddenly found himself alone on the concrete basketball court with both hands covering his head. He sat up and could immediately feel the cuts and bruises, which he was accustomed to from other altercations.

Sam just sat there. He could still see a few of the guys who had run out of fear of him in the distance. Then he heard a voice behind him.

"Hey, Moore." someone said.

When he turned around, he saw three older guys approaching him. He pushed himself up from the court and then stood up.

"Yeah?" he asked while brushing himself off.

"Aren't you tired of this? Always getting roughed up." one guy asked.

"What's it to you?" asked Sam.

"Don't let these young'uns keep getting the best of you. You don't need to be running with them. The big dogs like us, we don't do drama. Let us know if you want to be about that, alright?" he asked Sam.

Sam felt uncomfortable standing in front of the tough-looking guys who neared his size. He really didn't know what to say to the guys, so he just nodded his head to them as they walked on past the park. Ever so slowly, he walked over to where his basketball had rolled beside the goalpost and picked it up. Sam held the ball in both hands and looked at what he considered to be the closest thing to an avenue of success he would ever find. As he stood there a heavy feeling flooded over him. He realized that even while he was doing the one thing he truly loved and was good at, bad things still happened just as they did with everything else in his life. Sam felt angry with himself. In a fit of ever-increasing frustration, he threw the ball at the basketball goal backboard with full force and began to walk back toward home.

Though they were not so close in distance, Sam felt very close to Coach Jackson. However, he had no idea that they were both experiencing deep frustration at the exact same moment in time.

Coach David Jackson, who lived in the suburbs outside of Clear View, sat alone in his home on that late Saturday morning staring at his television screen. Though he was looking at the screen, his mind was in no way focused on it. He was so deeply frustrated with himself and was growing tired of his own company. He thought about calling his old college friend, Daniel Simmons, with whom he had recently reconnected. However, he still felt too ashamed at not being able to make the most of the coaching opportunity Daniel had worked out for him. He decided not to make the call and wondered if their relationship would shift back to a non-existent one. David realized his options to connect with anyone outside of a professional level were very limited now as his family was no longer there for him to lean on.

When it came to family, it had always been a complicated matter for David. He had brought the dysfunctional family traits that he had experienced growing up into his own family. Despite that, there had always been that one person who had been available and had supported him. It was a person who was always present in the background of his memories, but he had not taken time to welcome or want the companionship in the moment. He now understood how much he had taken for granted. David realized that he needed this person now more than ever.

David's reminiscing took him back to what had been a momentous day as a college athlete. It was his final home game at ESU. It was senior day and before tip-off, the seniors were to be escorted onto the court by their family members. For most of his fellow seniors, the family members included a father, mother, and possibly a sibling; but David had a much different situation. Having lost his father, who he could barely remember, and his mother, who had recently died after a long battle with cancer, David's lone escort was Beth. His wife of nearly two years at that point was who he considered to be family. To David that was just fine. She was all the family he wanted. He had no siblings, and his relationship with others connected to his mother and father had grown distant.

As the two of them walked onto the court to the sound of applause, David found himself looking up to a section in the bleachers that he had always tried to avoid during home games. He made direct eye contact with the man he knew as Uncle Joe. He sat in the same spot during every ESU basketball game, never missing a single one. Even in David's early years as an underclassman with very limited playing time, Uncle Joe was always there to show his support. Such a thing did not begin when David became a high school basketball star, it went back to his very first games as a young boy. If there was an athletic event in which David would be playing, everyone could count on Uncle Joe being there.

Joe Jackson was the brother of David's late father, but David had spent very little time with his father's family. Following the unexpected death of his father, he and his mother no longer attended any Jackson family events. Though they lived close by, nothing but pain and loss separated them. Growing up, David knew of the family and realized that he shared a last name with them. What he was not so clear about was the reason for such distance between them. David, never having received those answers, spent most of his life assuming the worst of the Jackson family. It was only after his mother became deathly ill and the Jacksons showed their support in many ways that the truth was revealed. To David, it all seemed much too late to openly receive what he had turned his back to all those years.

He continued the practice his mother had passed along to him by remaining separated from her own family after her passing. David was a very busy and newly married college athlete, and he used that as an excuse to exempt himself from family gatherings during his later days at ESU. He was determined to make his own path, and by senior day, his future aspirations seemed to be falling into place. Nearing a degree in sports and exercise science, a job opportunity was already lined up. His next move was to begin coaching at a middle school just outside of the college town. Beth would be starting her career as a math teacher at the same school. It was a start that allowed them to begin building a foundation that would later lead to a family.

The couple had an "us against the world" mindset as they walked arm in arm onto the court during David's senior day. Their thoughts were on nothing else but the future … their future. Nothing nor no one else was of any importance. However, for the brief second that David looked at Uncle Joe, his mind went to a place that he had a hard time escaping throughout every game. From Uncle Joe's seat in the bleachers, it had always been obvious to him that David ignored his presence at the games. At times it seemed as if his nephew was not even aware that he was there. David's senior day was Joe's final time watching him as an athlete. Uncle Joe had clearly noticed the eye contact that had been made with David and as the game went on, Joe felt he was too much of a distraction to his nephew.

After a rough first half for ESU, it did not help that their leading point guard, David Jackson, was off of his game. A one-sided halftime score in the other team's favor was the result of his many turnovers and missed shots. As the two teams headed to the locker rooms, Joe Jackson stood up and watched as David jogged off the court along with his teammates. The last thing Joe wanted to be was the distraction that ruined his nephew's senior day. As he made his way down the bleachers and headed towards the exit, Joe realized that could have very well been the last time seeing David … not only as a basketball player, but ever at all.

The ESU players came out of the locker room and began the second half with an entirely different mindset that led to better performance on the court. David regained his usual composure as the floor general, and led the team to a big comeback. As the second half's time began to expire, the score was tied. David found himself on the free throw line. His free-throw shots had always been a sure score; but with the game on the line, the pressure could have easily changed that. After taking a deep breath, he looked up to the goal with a clear mind and sent both shots straight through the net. After making the free throws, the game was only seconds from over. The opponent's only option was to heave the ball from past the half court line.

The ball did not even come close to the goal as the buzzer sounded, and ESU had finished their regular season on top. David and his fellow seniors were filled with euphoria as they celebrated their final win on the ESU home court. Amidst the celebration, David looked up to the bleachers that were still full of people. He decided to do the unthinkable and approach Uncle Joe, a man he hardly knew. Shifting his eyes up to his uncle's usual spot as more people came down from the bleachers, he saw that Uncle Joe was no longer there. David made his way over to the crowd of people cramming through the gym's exits in hopes of finding him. More and more loudly cheering people began to crowd around David as he tried to ease his way to the exit doors. It soon became impossible to move while comments such as *"good game!"* and *"you're amazing!"* were being shouted out by the supporters. David stopped and gave up any hope of finding Uncle Joe in the crowd of people. When he turned around to head toward the locker room, Beth was right in front of him. As he reached to embrace his wife, David had forgotten all about the people that surrounded them as well as his attempt to find his longest and most dedicated supporter.

The memory no longer seemed random. David knew exactly why his mind had taken him back to that point in time. The risky gamble he had made in traveling down a path that had steered him away from the one with whom he had started had finally back fired on him. Finding himself alone, his dreams in jeopardy with no family in sight, was a major contrast to the moment he had just revisited. David knew he had to make his way back to the road Beth was still traveling with their children. The only way to do so was to turn around and start from the beginning. Catching up to them would require some help, he thought. Support was desperately needed, and David could only think of one living person who had ever offered genuine interest in him. It was Uncle Joe, the man he had not given any thought to since the impulsive idea of finding him on his senior day. Before beginning the daunting task of finding his way back to Beth and his children, David had another road to travel, one that would be just as difficult … finding him.

Chapter 15

David rose to his feet as he suddenly remembered a way that he might be able to track down Uncle Joe … the Jackson family update. His cousin, who was the daughter of Uncle Joe, always wrote an annual family update and sent out to every member of the Jackson family around Christmas time. It was a tradition that had gone on for years as a way for everyone to stay informed about the many people in the family who were scattered all around the state. Though David had no type of contact with his family members, the update was still sent to his address each year. He had never taken any interest in reading them even though his recent Clear View coaching accomplishments had been heavily featured in the last update. David always left it up to Beth to either read it or just simply throw it away. He knew that Beth was not one to throw things like that away, and he had an idea where the update just might be.

David went up the stairs leading to the crowded attic. He stepped carefully around boxes to approach the area in the open space where the Christmas items were kept. After opening a few boxes, David's eye caught what he thought may be that for which he was searching. It was an open box full of Ziploc bags which held the Christmas cards they received in the past years. After grabbing the most recent bag he could find, David went back downstairs and dumped all of the cards out on the living room coffee table. The family updates were easy to spot among the other Christmas cards by the kind of paper on which they were printed and the design that resembled an essay. David sat on the edge of the couch cushion and looked at the year printed on the top of each page. The most recent one he found was two years old.

He enjoyed a brief moment of pleasure at seeing his name near the top of the page with the subject line noting his first state championship as a head basketball coach. David found himself looking through each of the other family updates to find his name, but he stopped short when he remembered his purpose for having them out of the attic. He skimmed through the most recent update to find any information on Uncle Joe. He felt sure Uncle Joe would be prominently featured since his daughter was the one who had had done all of the work on it. Near the end of the update, David finally spotted his name and found exactly what he needed. It read, "*My father, Joe Jackson, went through a big change this year. Since Mama's death, he had no interest in moving near us and did not want to leave his hometown: so we decided to move him into Clear View's local senior living facility.*"

Bingo! David thought. He knew exactly where the facility was located. He passed right by it almost every day when he went to the gym. David stood up and reached for his truck keys. With the cards still scattered on the coffee table, he headed out the door. An impulsive feeling had lit a spark within him to seek out something bigger than himself. David left his house to begin his newfound desire for mending the pieces of his life that he had been responsible for breaking.

It was only a few minutes later, when David found himself turning into the senior living facility parking lot, that he truly thought about just how close Uncle Joe had been all of these years. What David did not know was that they had actually been in the same building together in recent years. He was aware that his Uncle Joe had been in the stands for his nephew's Clear View coaching debut as well as for a few other games that season. It was not until his wife became sick and his own health had begun to decline that his appearances outside of home became very limited. His condition had eventually led him to the point of entering the same doors David was about to open at the senior living facility. This was the place life had now cornered him into calling home.

David pressed the red button beside the front entrance doors of the building and waited a few seconds after hearing a beeping sound.

A voice came through the intercom and asked, "May I help you?"

"Uh-yes. I'm here for a visit. Joe Jac-"

"Okay come on in." The voice said as the doors unlocked before he had a chance to finish saying his uncle's name.

As David entered into the facility, he sensed a very warm and calm atmosphere that made it seem to be a welcoming retreat. He approached the podium that was just to the left of the front entrance where a worker stood expecting him.

"Hello, sir. Welcome." said the lady.

"Hi." David replied.

"You're here for a visit?" she asked.

"Yes … yes, I am." he said.

"Name and relationship to the resident?" the lady asked.

"My name?" asked David, beginning to feel a bit nervous.

She clarified, "Name of the resident you're visiting, sir."

"Right, of course. I'm here to see Joe Jackson." David said.

"And your relation?" she asked.

In a soft tone, David replied, "I-I'm his nephew."

"Okay. You said Joe Jackson?" she asked as she scanned through the papers in front of her.

"Yes." replied David.

"Hmm, I'll be back in one moment." the lady said as she took one of the papers with her.

While David stood there and waited, he thought about the ambitious task that had originally seemed nearly impossible. The idea that had come to him less than an hour before … finding someone he had not paid any mind to in decades. He had not thought it would be this easy. Yet here he was! It was only a matter of minutes now before his quick thinking would pay off. David was hopeful that this efficient plan was a sign that things would continue to fall into place in a quick manner. With all these thoughts rolling over in his mind, he continued to take in the view of the building's interior. He peaked his head inside the library and sitting room area, which was just to the right of the front entrance. Seeing a couple of gentlemen residents sitting in the room, he nodded his head at them before he heard the lady's voice from behind him.

"Sir." she said.

David turned around to see that a man dressed in a business suit was standing beside her. He walked over to them and could immediately tell that something was not right by the looks on their faces.

"I'm the manager here. I was just informed that you were here to see Joe Jackson." the man said.

"Yes, that's right. Is there a problem?" asked David.

"Well, Sir, I'm not exactly sure how to tell you this; but Mr. Jackson is no longer with us." the man said.

"Oh, so he moved off somewhere else?" David asked, thinking now that his plans would become more complicated.

"Well, not exactly. Mr. Jackson had a heart issue and was transported to the hospital, and"

David's voice began to break as he interrupted, "I-I see. He's at the hospital?" He hoped his Hail Mary of a question would bring the answer he wanted.

"Sir," the man said, as he picked up where he was interrupted, "And we were informed that Mr. Jackson passed away."

Shock surged through David's being as he heard the gentleman say those words. His hopes for a promising outcome were completely depleted. What had felt like an occurrence of fate had now been exposed as a dirty trick that he could only believe the universe would play on him. To get so seemingly close to the connection and support for which he finally yearned, was yet another slap in the face. He stood there feeling as if he was in another realm of the cruel reality from which he had always tried to keep himself.

To gain more clarity, David asked the man, "Was this recent?"

The man behind the podium thought to himself for a moment and answered, "It's been several months."

Hearing that caused David to realize just how much distance he had created from his family. He was not even aware of his Uncle's death that had happened two months ago. Finding himself in this embarrassing situation, a feeling of anger toward his family came over him. He began to think, "*How could they?*" However, in the next moment, he admitted to himself that he really had no right to blame anyone other than himself.

The man behind the podium, unsure of the right words to say in a situation like this, spoke up. "I'm so … We're so sorry that you had to find out this way, sir."

David just stood there … remaining still with no response.

The gentleman asked, "Sir, is there anything we can do for you?"

Filled with inner shame, "Oh-no. No. Wow, I'm sorry." said David as he noticed the dramatic scene he was beginning to create.

"No worries, sir." the gentleman responded.

When David saw the man leave the podium to get on with his day, David realized that he had no choice but to do the same thing.

Just as he took a few steps back and turned around to open the door, another voice came from behind him, "Hold up one second."

David turned back around to see an older gentleman with a cane slowly coming toward him from behind where the woman was standing by the podium.

"Joe. Joe Jackson … you knew him?" the man asked David as he continued to approach him.

"Yes, but clearly not well enough." David replied.

"Ah, I knew him." the older gentleman said as he stood in the doorway between the library and sitting room. "Knew him real well."

"Yeah?" asked David.

"Yep." the man replied, as he turned and walked slowly into the sitting room.

David was suddenly intrigued by the old man and was expecting something more from him. He looked at the lady at the podium as a way of asking permission to follow the man. The lady, who had watched as David received the tough revelation, gave him a thumbs up to go ahead. He walked into the sitting room and noticed that the two men who had been there minutes earlier had left. The old man took a seat in a chair over to the side of the room, sat his cane aside and reached for a newspaper from the table.

"Do you mind if I come in?" asked David, who by then was standing in the doorway.

"Oh ... Come on in. Take a seat." the man said, "As you can tell, when you get to a certain age, you just let people come to you."

"I see that." David said as he walked in and sat on the couch across from the old man.

As the gentleman took his glasses from his shirt pocket and unfolded the newspaper, David asked, "So you knew him well, huh?"

With the newspaper in front of his face, the man replied, "Oh yeah."

"Wish I could say the same." David replied, "I'm the one who still thought he was alive."

The man placed the newspaper on his lap and said with a chuckle, "I'll tell ya, he was one of only a few people I liked around this place."

David was not sure where to start. He had so many questions he wanted to ask. They all began to crowd his mind, but the old man starting asking him questions.

"You gotta name, young man?" he asked him.

"Yeah. Yeah, it's David ... David Jackson." he replied.

"I'm Clarence Henderson." the old man said as he reached his hand out for a shake but did not in any way lean forward.

David got up from the couch across from Clarence and reached over to shake his hand.

"I guess you did have a connection to Joe, having the same last name is a pretty strong one." said Clarence.

"That doesn't tell the whole story." David replied.

"I know it doesn't, because I know the story ... I've heard it before."

"You-you have?" asked David.

"Well, yeah. What do you think your *Uncle* Joe and I would talk about?" Clarence asked.

Hearing him specify "uncle" impressed David, and he replied, "So you have heard of the story."

"I've heard of you too ... Coach." Clarence said as he lowered his glasses.

Before David could bring himself to say anything more in response, a nurse entered the room. "There you are, Mr. Henderson." she said, "I'm sorry to interrupt, but it's time for your shower."

Clarence put the newspaper back on the table and reached for his cane. The nurse came closer to attempt to help him, but he waved his hand and refused any assistance. Clarence let out a grunt as he slowly stood up from the couch. David remained seated while watching, still unsure of what to do or say. Clarence gave him a pat on the shoulder as he made his way out of the sitting room, and David turned around to watch him follow behind the nurse.

David was left in awe of the man he had just met. While processing the knowledge he had stumbled across, he realized the potential that came along with it. David was already transfixed on what Clarence had yet to share with him. He could just imagine so many things of value inside of Clarence's head, and he was filled with an urge to get them out.

That urge led him back to the same place the very next day. David pressed the red button and was admitted to the facility. It was late Sunday morning. He noticed a different lady behind the front entrance podium. He felt a sense of relief in avoiding being remembered from the awkward scenario of the day before.

"Hello, sir. Please state the name of the resident you are here to visit." she said.

David replied with the name he had made sure not to forget, "Clarence Henderson."

The lady asked, "Mr. Henderson, you said?"

"Yes." replied David.

"As in *Clarence* Henderson?" she asked, sounding surprised.

"Yes, unless I was given a fake name." said David.

"No, no that's his name. It's just very rare for him to get visitors." the lady said.

"Really?" David asked.

"Yes. I can't ever remember anyone being here to see him. How do you know him?"

David thought for a moment and replied, "Um, he's a friend of a friend. I just recently met him."

"That explains it, I guess." she said, "What's your name, sir?"

"David Jackson."

"Okay, Mr. Jackson. I'll get one of the nurses to let him know that you're here. Feel free to take a seat."

"Thank you." He replied as she walked away.

David headed over toward the sitting and library room where he randomly pulled a book from the shelf and took a seat on the same couch where he had sat the day before. With his back to the room's entrances, he looked down and began to scan through the book in his lap.

Clarence was doing a similar thing from inside of his room, except the book on his lap was titled, *The Holy Bible.* His television was on the channel that showed church services on Sunday mornings. While his index finger followed along during the reading of a verse, Clarence's intercom suddenly buzzed.

"Mr. Henderson." said the voice.

"What?" asked Clarence, "It's not time for me to go anywhere or do anything, is it?"

"No, sir. But you do have a visitor."

"Just tell her to leave the payment check at the front like usual." Clarence replied.

"It's a gentleman named David Jackson. He's here to see you. Is it not a good time?"

Clarence was suddenly staggered as he said, "Oh. Well, uh. That's fine! Just give me a minute."

Back in the sitting room where David remained waiting, the book with which he had quickly grown bored was on the table in front of the couch. His patience was waning, and he found himself constantly glancing back to check the time. He knew this was due to the eagerness and anticipation he felt. He decided to get up from the couch and walk back to the front lobby area. As he was walking out of the sitting room, he nearly ran into Clarence who had slowly made his way down the long hall to meet him.

"Leaving already?" asked Clarence.

"Oh, no. Not at all. I was just checking to see if you were coming, but here you are." said David as he backed into the sitting room.

"Here I am." said Clarence as he took a seat on the couch. "What brings you back?"

"Uh, well." David said in response to the unexpected question.

"What are you running from?" Clarence asked.

"I'm sorry?" David replied to the unexpected question. "*What am I running from?*" he echoed.

"You must be running from something for you to come back here to this place and want to see me." said Clarence.

David was still flustered and unable to come up with any response.

Clarence asked him, "Is it loneliness? Do you have a family back home?"

"Mr. Henderson, if you don't mind, I figured that I could ask *you* a few questions." said David, avoiding the question that he had been asked.

"So you're running *towards* something. Answers maybe?" replied Clarence.

"Yeah, sure. I guess so." David replied.

"I'm sorry to dump all of these kinds of questions on you. It was just talked about in the sermon that I was watching."

"Oh yeah?" asked David in an attempt to sound interested in the sermon subject.

"Yeah. I can also relate to doing a whole lot of running in my own life. Not literally, as you can tell." Clarence said as he placed his hand on his belly.

"Really ... what were *you* running from." David asked him.

"Ah, I see what you did there with getting your question in." Clarence said with a laugh, "But that's alright ... I'm not afraid to answer. Not anymore."

David, defending himself, said, "Now, sir, I'm not afraid, I just-"

"You just have a fear of *being* afraid. That'll get you every time ... a fear of anything other than God's will. My fear led me to start running."

"Where to?" asked David.

"Jail." Clarence bluntly replied with a laugh.

David asked, "Well, then I guess the real question is where from?"

Clarence was not as quick to respond this time and took a moment before doing so. After letting out a deep and seemingly painful breath, he replied in a regretful tone, "From love, commitment ... eventually my own family."

David had no response. He could only think of himself and his own circumstances that were being described by the man he was facing.

Clarence continued, "Anyways, it was a long and messy journey that led me here. The only connection I have with family is a payment check that my ex-wife sends to keep me here."

"That's a shame. I mean, it's good that she does that but-" David muttered.

"Look, son. Don't have pity for me." Clarence said as he broke in. "Don't feel bad for me like this was all out of my control. It wasn't. It was of my own doing. It was years' worth of mistakes that eventually caught up with me."

David replied, "I think it takes courage to admit that, sir."

"Well, I eventually learned to accept and own up to all of it. I wish I had done it much sooner because time eventually makes some things unrepairable. I can hardly even stand to face my ex-wife anymore because I can still see the pain in her eyes ... pain that *I* caused." he paused for a moment. He continued, "But fixing yourself doesn't change everything. What begins real change is finding something to fight *for* in life. I spent too much time fighting *against* my own issues. It wasn't until I was confined to the inside of these walls that I could see that."

"It's not too late, though. There's always time." said David.

"That's an easy thing for a young guy like yourself to say." Clarence told the middle aged man. "As you can tell, there ain't a whole lot of time left for me." he continued as he held up his cane to draw attention to his having to use it.

"So what are you fighting for now?" asked David.

"Many things. Some days it's as simple as strength to leave my room; but more importantly, I'm fighting for moments like these ... opportunities to share experiences ... to make connections." said Clarence.

David realized more than Clarence could possibly know about how much of a relatable connection they shared. As he listened to Clarence talk, a sense of fear settled in his mind as he imagined the worst case scenario of his own future.

Clarence asked him, "And you?"

David, distracted from his thoughts, replied, "I'm sorry?"

"What are you fighting for? If you don't mind me getting in one question." said Clarence.

David didn't mind the question. He was just not sure of how to answer it. The honest truth was that he had no idea.

Chapter 16

Around 4 months later

The first month of the school year still felt fresh to David even though it had passed quickly. He found himself as athletic director due to a surprise promotion over the summer. It was the best thing for him as the new responsibilities allowed his focus to be on all aspects of the school's athletic department. David understood that the added job title could not have come at a better time. In what would have been a long and dismal summer for him, he had actually spent it hard at work in preparation for Clear View's fall sports. During that time of year, he had always been the one who went to work because of a desperate desire to be occupied away from personal obligations back at home. The new job had managed to come at a time when his life at home had changed drastically. Elijah and Molly were only there every other weekend and one night during the week. On the mornings that the house was empty, David realized his subconscious call to leave the house was not as loud and urgent as it used to be. This had been especially true during the early weeks of the summer break prior to his new job assignment. He had struggled then to adjust his life to an open schedule.

David had ended the previous school year feeling very uneasy because of the lack of talent he had observed during the basketball workouts. It had left him with little desire to look forward to the next season's team. Now, at this transitional season of his life, there was one bright spot that David had begun to enjoy on his free days. It was his frequent visits with Clarence Henderson at the senior living facility. David eventually had every opportunity to learn all about his Uncle Joe. He felt that he had come to know him well through the stories Clarence told him. Between visits, David jotted down many questions to ask and thoughts to discuss with Clarence. He eventually started taking a tape recorder with him. He would sit it on the table between the two couches in order to capture Clarence's priceless way of slowly recounting memories. David often found himself almost entranced while Clarence talked. The subject matter and tone of his voice took David into another world during each visit. But eventually, the trips to that special place became less frequent.

David had a new sense of enthusiasm since that random summer day when he had received that special call from Principal Wallace. He had asked David to come right away to his office at Clear View High School. When David arrived, he saw a long-time teacher and assistant football coach in the office. He was the one who had served as the school's athletic director for nearly thirty years. Principal Wallace explained to David that they had discussed a change in the athletic director position. David's fellow teacher and coach was ready to relinquish the AD job, and had asked Principal Wallace to release him. He was getting ready to leave the office, but waited to hear Principal Wallace discuss the position with David. "You're the man for this position. You are the true representation of Clear View athletics." Principal Wallace said, as the other man nodded his head in agreement. That was all it took for David to accept.

When David arrived at work the following day, he soon noticed many new items that had shown up on his desk, none of which had to do with basketball. David placed the title and priorities of "athletic director" in front of "coach." He felt very good that, throughout all of the changes at home and at work, he was still beloved by everyone on the Clear View campus as the new school year began. David was still known as "Coach Jackson" or "Coach Jack" to every student, player, and staff member at the school. Knowing that and enjoying the students that filled the hallways every day lessened the concern he felt about the basketball coaching job.

Early on a Monday morning, David was off to a head start in preparing for his physical education classes for the day. With still nearly a half an hour before the school day was to begin, his desk phone rang.

"Yes?" David said when he picked it up.

"Coach Jackson, it's Principal Wallace here."

David, who expected the school secretary to be on the line, cleared his voice and replied, "Oh. Hey, Sir. Good Morning."

"Would you mind coming by my office for a second?" said Principal Wallace.

"Oh, sure. I'll be right there."

David slowly hung up the phone wondering what the purpose might be for the rare visit with Principal Wallace. The last time David had been in his office was when he learned about his added position as athletic director. He headed up to the front office and was greeted by several other teachers who were making their way toward the classrooms to start their day.

When David knocked on Principal Wallace's door, he was told, "Come on in."

Principal Wallace wiped his mouth and put his empty cereal bowl aside.

"Close the door, if you don't mind." he said to David.

After David did so, Principal Wallace motioned for him to sit. As he took a seat, Principal Wallace spoke up, "Basketball season will be here before you know it."

"You're right." responded David. "Hard to believe." he continued, knowing that he could soon no longer avoid it.

"You know a young man named Sam Moore, right?" asked Principal Wallace.

"Oh, yes Sir. He showed up to some basketball workouts, and I see he is already on the varsity football team."

"*Was* on the varsity football team." Principal Wallace said, lifting his eyebrows.

"Was? What happened?" asked David.

Principal Wallace sat up in his chair and folded his hands on his desk before speaking. "Well, Sam has had a few scuffles in practices; but during Friday's game, he got into a big fight. Punches were thrown, and he even started swinging at his own guys when they tried to break it up."

"So as athletic director, do I need to fill out some type form on this matter?" asked David.

"I'm telling *you*, our head basketball coach, that Sam will not be on your team this year. I've heard that he's a mighty good basketball player, but there's just no way ... and I wanted to make you aware of that."

David, as he began to stand up, replied, "Don't worry. I was told this could happen. I was expecting it, but thanks for letting me know, Sir."

"Have a good day, Coach." Principal Wallace said as David opened the door and left the office.

David was without any answers or direction for the upcoming season, but he had no choice but to begin to prepare for it. Walking back to the gym, he did his best to maintain the outgoing personality for which he was known. He got back to his office and broke the news to Marshal. Like David, he was in no way surprised. It was still crushing to both of them. Even though they had known this could happen, they each had desperately hoped for a good outcome that would allow Sam Moore to be on their team. Now that seemed impossible.

The school day was already off to a rocky start, and the thought of the troubled young man with loads of potential would not leave David's mind. After first period ended, he stood outside the gym doors for his usual hallway duty. The halls were packed with moving students, but there was one group ahead of him that caught his attention. Right in the middle of the group was Sam Moore whose height made him easy to spot. Sam was on his way to his second period class when a trio of upperclassmen approached him.

"Hey, Moore." one of them said,

Sam turned around, "Yeah?"

"We saw what happened Friday night."

"And?" Sam snorted as he became defensive and made his way closer to him.

The boy replied, "Woah!" as he raised his hands. "We don't want any of that action with you. We figured that you might want some with us after school. We have something that should calm you down a bit."

"What are you trying to say?" asked Sam.

"We're trying to say that you probably have nowhere to be, nothing to do. Live a little. You know where to find us after school." the boy said as he and the two others in the group walked away.

Though Sam was bigger in size, he was outmatched by the three guys. There was an intimidation factor that the older guys successfully portrayed. It was something David could clearly see from where he stood across the hall; and although he had not heard what was said, he was able to read between the lines of the interaction. Something about the scene sparked a possible solution which gave David the urge to step in. The three guys were out of sight and among the crowd of students as Sam continued walking to his next class. David came from behind him and made sure to get his attention without triggering Sam in any way.

"Mr. Moore." David said.

Sam heard the voice and knew only an adult would address him in that manner. He turned around and saw Coach Jackson giving him the beckoning sign with his index finger. Sam followed Coach Jackson, and they stopped a few feet apart from everyone else in the hall.

"You okay, son?" asked David.

"Yeah, I'm straight." replied Sam as he broadened his shoulders.

"Good, so you can meet me after school in the gym for a workout?" asked David.

"Y'all are still doing those?" Sam asked.

"*You* could be." David said. "I see you have some basketball shoes on now. I've got a change of clothes you can play in and a vehicle to take you home. What do you say?"

"Alright. I'll be there." Sam said.

"Come straight to the gym when the bell rings. Now you go straight to your second period classroom."

Sam nodded his head as he quickly made his way down the emptying hallway. He was just able to make it to class on time. When the school day ended, he was right back at the gym doors to meet Coach Jackson. David saw him and met him carrying a practice jersey along with a pair of basketball shorts.

"Change into these." David said, handing them over to Sam. "You have five minutes."

Sam jogged into the locker room and made it back just in time as David stood beside the ball rack with his phone timer going. His main focus was to instill a sense of discipline in the young man who seemed to need it desperately. David knew that if Sam could make it through this workout, things would be looking up. Sam spent the first few minutes stretching; and to his surprise, Coach Jackson began the workout with full court sprints. The beginning portion of the workout lasted much longer than Sam had anticipated. He did not pick up a basketball for the first half of the workout. What he thought would just be a basic shoot around was in fact a *workout*.

After Sam's time alone on the court with Coach Jackson edged over an hour, David saw the sweat that dripped off Sam's skin and figured it was a good time to end.

"Alright." David said while looking at his watch after Sam completed the final drill. "Let's call it for today. Go on in there and change, I'll be out here waiting."

"Five minutes!" Sam said, breathing heavily.

"Five, eh … I'll give you six." David said as Sam began to slowly jog off the court.

When Sam came out with the soaking wet jersey and shorts in his hand, David was standing by the door and ready to go.

"Just toss those in the laundry room, I'll get them washed tomorrow." said David.

They both headed out the door and began walking toward David's truck. While they walked in the parking lot, the football team could be seen and heard as they practiced in the distance. David trailed behind Sam and noticed him looking in their direction with obvious disappointment.

To put Sam's focus elsewhere, David said, "It's that truck right straight ahead."

After getting in and leaving the school campus, they sat in silence as the radio played. David then turned the radio volume all the way down.

After they were out on the road, David spoke up, "So, Sam, tell me about yourself."

"I'm pretty sure people have already told you everything about me." Sam replied.

"Well, I've heard about the things you've done, not about who you are." said David.

Sam took a moment for what Coach had said to sink in, and then he said, "I don't think there's much difference between the two."

"That's not totally true." David replied, "I don't think a person should determine who they are based on the things they've done in the past."

"But I just got kicked off another team *today*." said Sam.

"That's in the past. It already happened. Tell me, Sam, what are you doing right now at this moment?" asked David.

"Uh, sitting in your truck, on the way home."

"On the way home from what?" David asked.

"Playing basketball?" Sam replied with a questionable look toward David.

"It wasn't just playing basketball. I mean, you love playing basketball right?"

"Yeah, I do." Sam nodded as he spoke.

David asked Sam, "But what else did you do?"

"Well." Sam said, "You had me do all of those sprints. I didn't love that."

"So, you not only did something you love, but you did something that wasn't easy and got through it." said David with enthusiasm.

"Well, I guess so, yeah."

"And you know what?" asked David.

"What?"

David replied, "You didn't have to do any of it."

"What do you mean?" Sam asked.

"When I told you to do those sprints, you could have looked me dead in the eye and said no, then walked off the court. There would have been nothing I could do. What you did was voluntary. It was *you* who chose to stick with it."

Sam replied with a low voice, "That's true."

"I think that says a lot about who you are and who I believe you can be." David said to him.

When they eventually pulled into Sam's driveway, David asked him, "Same thing tomorrow?"

Without any hesitation, Sam replied, "I'll be there." Before closing the passenger side door, he said, "Thanks a lot, Coach."

While David watched Sam enter his house, the thought of coaching suddenly felt fresh again. Though there were many challenges ahead for the next season, one much bigger than basketball had introduced itself, and David openly welcomed it. He knew, however, that there was something that needed to be addressed before facing such a task. With that thought in mind, he headed back to the Clear View High campus. David parked in the lot in front of the building and used his staff card to enter through the school's main entrance. Without skipping a beat, he headed straight o the front office and toward Principal Wallace's door.

"Well, hello, Coach Jackson." the secretary said when she saw David making his second visit of the day to the office.

"Is Mr. Wallace in?" asked David as he continued to walk toward his office.

"Yes, but he's finishing up with a call." she said.

All David heard was her "yes" … and before hearing her full response, David was already opening Principal Wallace's office door. He looked up at David with surprise as he was ending his phone conversation. David softly closed the door and remained standing while waiting.

When Principal Wallace hung up the phone he half-jokingly said to David, "Coach, there better be a good reason why you came in here the way you did."

"I apologize for my entry, but there is." David replied with a look and tone of seriousness.

"Oh. Well, alright. What's up?" asked Mr. Wallace.

"I don't think I can continue as athletic director." David said.

"You don't? Why is that? I thought you would really like it."

"I do, but I think there's something that needs my full focus and attention." replied David.

"Basketball? It wouldn't be hard to delegate certain tasks to Coach Lee." Mr. Wallace suggested.

"Not just basketball." David said as he took a seat. "I think Sam Moore has a chance."

"Ugh." Mr. Wallace said as he sat back in his chair, "Now coach, we've already talked about this."

"I just spent time with him. I think if we put him in the right situations, he can straighten out."

"There's more to it than that, David. You're dealing with a different beast here. His behavior isn't the only problem. The kid is failing math and is very close to doing so in his other classes." Mr. Wallace said sternly.

"So we're just going to let him? Is that how this works? The boy needs some help and I'm trying to give it to him."

"There's only so much you, I, or anyone else can do for him. He has to decide to help himself, and he's proven many times that he doesn't want to."

David asked, "Does he not want to? Or is he unable to?"

"Nobody knows the answer to that." Mr. Wallace said, "The boy is a closed book."

"Has anyone ever even tried to open it? Did they slam it back shut after a few pages? Sir, would you at least let me try and find the answer?" asked David.

"Look, getting him straightened out behavior wise is the first step of many. He still would be nowhere close to academically eligible for the start of basketball season which is in less than two months."

"I can live with that. Just trust me." David said.

Mr. Wallace leaned forward and thought for a moment. He then asked, "Coach, why are you doing this?"

David took a moment before responding. "I don't have an exact answer to that. I think there's many reasons why, which gives me more assurance that this is the right move."

"Alright, alright. I trust you. I'll get his files together for you to see what you're working with. Don't let this come back and bite you."

Leaving the office, David knew deep down in his heart what the real answer to Principal Wallace's question was … he had found something to fight for.

Chapter 17

When David arrived back at Clear View the next day, he found Sam's academic files in the mailbox on the coaching office door. When he sat down at his desk to take a look at them, it was clear that Principal Wallace was not exaggerating about Sam's struggles in school. David saw that his grade in math was much lower than the other lackluster ones. He suddenly had a thought as he was taking a closer examination of Sam's performance in that class. It appeared that he was not a good test taker and that his participation in other assignments was not making up for it. David's first thought went to Beth. She had been his wife of over twenty years and was once a math teacher herself at the eighth-grade level even though she had just recently changed careers. After their separation, their communication had been limited only to things related to their children, Elijah and Molly. They had worked together on matters such as their schedules and times to get the children for custody purposes.

Still, David knew it was worth asking Beth. "Surely math hasn't changed *that* much." David said to himself as he thought of the long-stretched possibility that she could help Sam. He knew the best time to do so, as opposed to calling out of the blue, would be the coming Friday when he was to pick up the kids for the weekend. Before that would happen, David knew that there was much to do in the busy week that was just beginning. Each day consisted of teaching his physical education classes, preparing Sam's afternoon workouts, and constantly checking in on him. David's main priority was to make it known to Sam that his office was an open door for him to view as a safe space. David reminded Sam of that every day during their drive to Sam's house after the tough workout he completed each afternoon. David was not so sure that Sam really understood that offer. Each time it was mentioned, he responded with a simple, "Okay." in his usual low, deep-toned voice.

David could see how so many people gave up on their attempts to get Sam to open up about any troubles he had. He seemed to want to cover them beneath many thick layers. However, David's persistence would soon pay off and would even catch Sam completely off guard. One of the few things Sam did make David aware of was a math test that would take place at the end of the week. Knowing this allowed David to keep Sam's schedule open on Thursday afternoon to prepare for the test that would be taken the next day. Sam got as far as opening up his math notebook, which was hardly filled out, and scanning through one single page. The few formulas that were written down seemed like a foreign language to him. It was something that he had no interest in learning. Feeling so, he made a quick decision to not study.

Sam sat at his desk the next morning of first period math. Now seeing the test, he regretted his decision. There was not a single question that he could answer with confidence. He left most of the non-multiple choice questions nearly blank. What made matters worse was seeing every other classmate seemingly know what to do. As they used their calculators and were hard at work, all he could do was watch. His self-induced frustration began to brew and carried over into his second period class. It was a sigh of relief for all of the students when they saw a substitute teacher waiting for them in that classroom. It signaled that their Friday would be spent taking it easier than most normal days. Sam pulled out his headphones and blasted music into his ears as he walked in and took his seat at the back of the classroom.

The substitute teacher greeted the class and began to call names from the attendance sheet. She got half way down the list and called out, "Samuel Moore?"

There was no answer from Sam, and everyone in the class, knowing he was there, turned around to face him and get his attention.

"Samuel Moore? Is he not here?" she asked.

Sam noticed everyone looking at him and removed his head phones.

"What?" he forcefully asked.

"Are you Samuel?" the substitute teacher asked.

Sam, already feeling testy, took no pleasure in hearing many of his classmates begin to laugh at hearing his birth name repeated several times.

"No." Sam said loud and clear. "I'm Sam."

"Sam. Okay, on here it just says Samuel."

The laughs within the class continued and grew louder.

"Okay, well I'm telling you that I'm Sam. Want me to spell it out?"

"That will not be necessary, young man." she replied.

"S-A-M." Sam said sarcastically slow.

"I'm glad we're making a big deal out of your name. One day I'll be sure to look it up in the county jail." the substitute teacher said.

Everyone in the class was loving the entertainment and turned around to see what Sam's reaction would be. When they saw the look on his face, the laughter stopped. They were aware of his angry outbursts; some were even frightened by it. It was a well-known fact that Sam could easily take offense to any given action or statement that he did not like. It was clear to those watching that the one he had just heard had hit him in a very fragile spot. His fellow students had no idea of his earliest memories in life, memories that included visiting family members at the jail or sitting in courtrooms with his grandmother for hours to show them support. He had vowed to never end up in such a place himself. Hearing an authority figure foretell his future in jail was the final push to send Sam over the edge.

His classmates could sense what was coming. They saw Sam's hands begin to shake as the rest of his body stiffened. While the substitute teacher continued calling the names on the class roster, Sam slowly stood up from his seat. He snatched up his book bag and glared at the substitute teacher at the front of the classroom. Sam could picture himself throwing the bag, which had some weight to it, and hitting her directly in the face. It would be so easy, he thought to himself as he held the book bag by one of the shoulder straps. Every head was turned in his direction and all eyes were on him. Each of the students grew more tense as they watched Sam sorting through the extreme thoughts going through his mind. The substitute teacher finished calling the names on the list and looked up to see Sam standing up at the back of the room.

"Young man, please take your seat." she said as she stared directly into the outraged expression on his face.

Sam heard none of it, but he could sense the anxiety rising within the class as nobody knew what would come next. He himself was unsure of what he would do as the indignation he felt had once again taken control of his mind and body.

"Sit down, young man!" the substitute teacher exclaimed in a louder tone.

While everyone looked at the teacher like she was crazy for pushing Sam's buttons that were not to be touched, the unexpected began to unfold. Sam's breaths suddenly became slower, his grip on the book bag loosened and he put each strap over his shoulders.

When Sam turned around and walked toward the door, she yelled from the front of the classroom, "I will write you up!"

Sam was fine with that and knew such a thing would be the best possible outcome of the situation. Without looking back, he slowly opened the door and made his exit from the classroom as his classmates took in the scene that had taken an unexpected turn. Sam walked down the empty hallway knowing there was only one place to go and one person with whom he could retreat. When he opened the gym doors to the sound of loud music playing on the speakers and basketballs bouncing, it was a chaotic scene to take in. Sam made his way through the many students that were enjoying their Friday free time. Some of them called him by name and asked him to join in their games. He paid no mind to them as he walked toward the coaching table and saw Marshal Lee on his laptop.

"Where's Coach Jackson?" Sam asked Marshal.

"In the office. You good?" Marshal asked Sam as he noticed the look on his face.

Sam left without answering. He approached the coach's closed office door. When he tried to turn the handle he found that the door was locked. Sam took a step back as his hostile nature was about at the blowing point. Balling up his fist, he could imagine the small glass window shattering from the wooden door. As he launched his right arm forward, the fog that clouded his judgement suddenly cleared just before he first made contact with the door.

The thought of what he had almost done brought him to tears as he turned his back and pressed his book bag against the door. Sam slid down and ended up seated on the floor. He tilted his head up and felt the tears shift their direction. Then he let out a scream that was muffled a bit by the carpeted hallway.

After a few seconds Sam heard two knocks on the door from behind him. He quickly stood up and tried to hide the tears on his face as the office door opened up. With his head facing down in embarrassment, he could only hope that it was David until he heard the familiar voice.

"That's all you had to do." David said, referring to the two knocks on the door.

"Sorry, coach." Sam replied with his head still down.

David asked, "What was all the commotion out here?"

Sam stood silently. He knew that saying a single word was all it would take for him to break down.

"It sounded familiar … almost like a cry for help." David said.

Sam began to nod his head when he felt David's fingers lifting up on his chin. As Sam's head lifted, his shame was released when he looked into Coach Jackson's eyes and heard him say, "I've been there before, Sam. There's a dent on my desk over there to prove it."

After pausing for a moment, David continued in a serious manner, "But I'm going to do everything I can to ensure that you'll never have to make that cry again."

Sam nodded as David reached out his hand for him to shake. With Sam's hand gripping his, he curiously asked David, "Did you say a dent?"

David grinned and motioned for Sam to walk with him over to his desk. He pointed to the dented middle desk drawer; and as they both observed it, David thought back to the moment it had happened.

"Man, I kicked the crap out of that thing. I was at my lowest point imaginable, but getting there allowed me to begin working my way back up again." David said.

"How far up have you gotten since then?" asked Sam.

David replied, "Not as far as I should be. There's a long way to go."

This came as a surprise to Sam, who thought Coach Jackson surely had his life all together based on the way that he carried himself.

"But the journey never ends." David continued as he looked at Sam, "And yours is just beginning."

David's journey continued even as the school day ended. Before picking up Elijah and Molly, he had a few hours open in his schedule on the Friday afternoon. In previous weeks as the athletic director, David had remained at the school for the home football games. If it was his weekend with the kids, Beth had dropped them off there and they had shadowed him for the entirety of the long games. It was a responsibility that David did not have to worry about anymore. He surprisingly felt relief at the weight off his shoulders when leaving the campus soon after the students were dismissed. David saw the few open hours he had as an opportunity to make a visit that was long overdue and much needed.

From the Clear View High campus, he drove into town and made his way back to the senior living facility for the first time since the beginning weeks of summer. Prior to the promotion, his trips had become such a routine occurrence that the facility workers all knew him. They recognized him when he was admitted and were glad to see him back after several months of absence.

"Well, there's Mr. Jackson." the familiar lady who was seated behind the front podium said as David walked in.

"Hey there." he replied, almost ashamed of how long it had been since visiting.

"We were getting a little worried about you around here." she said.

"Yeah, I bet. Things got pretty busy at work, but I'm here now."

"Well, I'm sure Mr. Henderson will be glad to see you. I'll get a call in to his room."

David awaited Clarence in the room where the two of them had shared so much. It was a space where he had unexpectedly learned much about himself, thanks to the familiar experiences that Mr. Henderson had gone through. Though their backgrounds were very different, certain similarities were much stronger and brought a real connection between the two men. Since so much time had gone by, David felt a little nervous as he remained standing close by the room's entrance.

"Hey there, stranger." said Clarence as he appeared.

David smiled as he gave a wave and nod to Clarence.

"Don't be so tense." Clarence said as his perceptive eye noticed David's awkward posture, "You don't have to reintroduce yourself, I remember you."

They both sat down across from each other, and Clarence began by simply asking, "How are you?"

"Well, busy to say the least."

"I understand that. How about your family?" Clarence asked.

"They're doing well; busy also. The kids are growing up."

"Now tell me, what's their names? I know you had told me before."

"Elijah and Molly." David replied, "I'm actually going to pick them up for the weekend from Beth's new apartment after our visit."

"That's great. How is she?" Clarence asked.

"Beth? Pretty good, as far as I know."

"Communication is very important when it comes to the mother of your children. It's much easier to lose than it is to gain back." said Clarence.

David replied, "I don't think I'll lose touch with her. I'm actually going to ask a big favor of her today."

Clarence asked, "A favor? Is that a good idea?" as he well remembered about David's shortcomings based on the honest stories he had heard from him.

"It's more for someone else than it is myself." said David.

"Oh yeah?" asked Clarence, who clearly wanted to know more.

"It's for this young fella I'm trying to help out. His name is Sam Moore. He's a freshman at Clear View."

"Is he a ball player?" asked Clarence.

David explained, "A really good one, but it's not looking like he'll be one of mine for this coming season. He has trouble in school, and I'm going to ask Beth if she would consider tutoring him in math."

"I'm sure it'll work out for the boy." Clarence said with optimism.

"His troubles aren't limited to subjects in school; it's much deeper than that." David continued.

"What's his deal?" asked Clarence.

"Anger." said David, "A whole lot of it."

Clarence slowly leaned forward and looked as if he was deep in thought with a hand placed on his chin.

"You know, it's funny you say that." Clarence said as he began to roll up his long sleeved shirt while David looked on with curiosity.

Clarence reached both arms out and exposed the scars that were clear to see on his dark skin. The scars that ran all the way down both his forearms and wrists.

"This is the result of pain that came from anger … a whole lot of it." Clarence honestly revealed.

David was unsure of how to respond. Clarence saved him from doing so as he continued, "I didn't take it out on myself first, it was my poor wife who got the worst of it. When I'd see her reaction, I would punish myself. The worst punishment of all was what it did to my kids. I passed that trait right on down to them."

"I just … don't know what to do. I don't know how to deal with anything like that." said David.

"I didn't know either!" Clarence replied, "I left my wife with two kids troubled with their own anger because *I* couldn't handle it. I could hardly even handle myself."

David said, "The only thing I feel like I can do is just be there for him, you know?"

"There's nothing more that you need to do." said Clarence. "The best thing for that boy is for you to stand there and listen. Just take it all in, nothing needs to be said."

"Do you have anyone to listen to you?" asked David.

"Well, yeah. I do right now, don't I?" Clarence replied with a smile, referring to how David had helped him without even being aware of it.

"But …" Clarence continued, "Most of the time there isn't anyone here to listen. Something that has helped when there's nobody around is to take a sheet of paper and write down anything and everything that is on my mind when I feel angry or lonely. It can even be written to someone, but the key is that it's for my eyes only ... nobody else's. I seal it in an envelope and keep it around in the open for a couple of days. Before I came here, I would just place it on an open fire. Since I can't burn anything around here, I have them all together stored in a box that I keep closed."

"And that helps?" asked David.

"Most definitely so, yes." replied Clarence.

David kept that in mind as he left the senior living facility and made the short trip to Beth's new apartment in town. It was his first trip there, and it took him a few minutes to find it in the large complex. David knocked on the door and found that it was unlocked when turning the handle.

"Knock knock." David said as he eased his way in and hoped it was the right apartment.

Beth appeared from around the corner and looked worn down as she replied, "Oh, come on in."

"You really should lock your door." said David.

"I've been going in and out all day while moving my things." she replied.

"It's a really nice place." David said as he looked around and tried to imagine it without so many moving boxes.

"That's the good thing about being in real estate now, I know when a good listing comes up. Plus, I was just ready to get out of my parents' house." Beth said.

"I can imagine that. Speaking of your parents, have they brought the kids here from school yet?"

"Yes. They're back there getting their things together. Oh! I forgot to mention that they both have sleepovers tonight." said Beth.

"Both of them? Tonight?" asked David with disappointment in his voice.

"Yeah. I'm sorry, but you should be able to pick them up tomorrow afternoon sometime. Here's the addresses for you to take them."

"*Great.*" David said. He then realized that the inconvenient news Beth had postponed sharing with him provided the perfect opportunity for him to ask something of her.

"Hey, I have a question." said David, "I know you've been very busy with work, but there's someone I know who needs serious help in math. Would you be willing to squeeze in a little time to work with him?"

"Someone as in?" asked Beth.

"Uh, his name is Sam Moore."

"Sam Moore? I think math should be the least of his concerns." Beth replied as she remembered hearing the countless number of terrible stories from her former middle school colleagues that taught him.

"Look, I know it seems bad; but I've spent enough time around the kid to see who he truly is outside of the classroom setting. Just give him a chance. Nobody else will. You're literally the last ounce of hope he has."

As soon as David said this, Elijah and Molly entered the room with their bags and were ready to go. Before leaving, David asked Beth, "Would you please just consider it?"

"I'll think about it, David." she replied.

"Think about what?" asked Molly.

Beth knelt down and looked at her daughter while saying, "Think about telling you to have a fun time and that Mom loves both of you." as she hugged both of the kids.

David picked up the kids' bags. "I'll be in the car." he said.

After delivering the kids to their respective sleepover houses, David soon found himself seated on his living room sofa, flipping through the television channels. What he had hoped would be a fun weekend with the kids had been cut short. He had no idea what to do with himself, it was in times such as this that David could not stand being alone. He flipped to a college football game that was not worth watching. He thought back to the conversation with Clarence that afternoon and what Clarence had shared near the end of their discussion. What David had originally heard his friend describe as a tool that could help Sam came to his mind. He wondered if it was a practice that might help him as well. He went over to the chair where he had dropped his work bag. He opened it and tore out a sheet of paper from one of the notebooks in it. With a pen in hand, David sat down at the kitchen table. He placed the blank sheet of paper in front of him. He took a moment to scan through his thoughts and determine what he should write. It only took a few seconds of reckoning before he realized that there was only one person on whom his thoughts were focused. It came as a surprise ... one that David could no longer deny ... which led him to put the ink to the paper and start the letter off by writing *Dear Beth*.

Chapter 18

David managed to make the most of his shortened weekend with the kids. He had grown a new appreciation for spending time with them since the separation. On Sunday evening when David saw Beth's car turning in the driveway, he told Elijah and Molly to go upstairs and gather their things. He quickly began to tidy up the living room area to make it more presentable before hearing the doorbell ring. As he took a second look around at the room, he ran his fingers through his tousled hair to improve his own appearance before he opened the front door.

"Hello." he awkwardly said, "Welcome."

"Hi." Beth replied as she made her way in. "The kids ready?"

"They're upstairs getting their things together." he replied.

"Okay. Well, I gave some thought to your request for me to work with Sam on his math." said Beth.

"Yeah?" asked David.

Beth let out a breath as she said, "I'll do it."

"Wow, Beth. That's really great. Thank you so much."

"*But* ..." she said with heavy emphasis, "I want you to understand that I'm not doing this to help you or your team. My help is only for a student who is struggling in math, that's it."

"Oh, yeah! That's completely fine. That is why I asked. This is only about Sam." David assured her.

"Okay, I'm glad we're on the same page." said Beth. "Let's schedule it for this coming Wednesday afternoon at five o'clock."

David replied, "Wednesday at five … that'll work."

Wednesday came very quickly, and it was business as usual when Sam met David in the gym after school for their usual afternoon workout. Once it was completed, instead of taking Sam home, David drove to his house for Sam to get freshened up before meeting with Beth. With his book bag in one hand and a sealed envelope containing his math scores from the semester in the other hand, Sam was ready for his tutoring. David could sense that Sam was a little nervous because he knew that Beth would remember him for his middle school years. Sam assured him that she was more than happy to help him. As Sam followed David through the front door, his eyes scanned the interior of the home.

David pointed to the hallway and said, "There's a shower down the hall to the right. Do you want a change of clothes?"

Sam replied, "Nah. I'm okay. I'll just wear what I had on at school, but thanks."

"Good." David said laughingly, "Because I really don't want those arms stretching my shirts."

While Sam made his way down the hall to the bathroom, David took a seat in his recliner. Leaning the seat back was all it took for him to start dozing off, and that was how Sam found him several minutes later when he came back into the room.

"Hey, Coach." Sam said to get David's attention.

"Oh, hey. You all freshened up?"

"Yes Sir, do you mind if we get a snack before we go?"

"Not at all." David said as he got up, "The kitchen is over here."

Sam picked up his book bag with his right hand and grasped the white envelope in his left hand and followed David to the kitchen. By the time he got into the kitchen, David was inside the walk-in pantry and was naming off the list of snacks available. Sam set his bag on the floor and placed the white envelope on the counter closest to the refrigerator. Looking around, it was obvious to Sam that it had been a while since the kitchen had been really cleaned. David had made space to put the snacks in the middle of several papers and folders that were on the counter. Sam pushed a folder aside in order to clear a space for the envelope which he was to take to Beth for the tutoring session. He took a seat on one of the stools and decided on a bowl of cereal for a snack. David took a seat beside him while he ate. It didn't take but just a few minutes for Sam to completely empty the bowl.

Sam wiped his mouth and then asked David, "So who is this that we're about to go see?"

"Beth Jackson. You might remember hearing about her at the middle school. She taught math while you were there."

"Yeah, Ms. Jackson. Is she your sister or something?" asked Sam.

"Oh, no." David replied, "She was my wife. We're separated now, but she was willing to help out."

"I see." said Sam, "I guess that's her with your kids over there." he said as he pointed to a nearby framed picture, one of the few in the house that included the four of them.

"Yeah. Yeah, that's her and my kids, Elijah and Molly." David replied as his eyes were fixed on the picture, "That's my daughter's favorite photo. The look on her face whenever she sees it is priceless, so I kept it out."

"And your son, does he play basketball?" asked Sam.

"Only through a video game console." said David. "I bought him a basketball game for it, and he's been teaching me how to use it as of late. What he doesn't know is that I sometimes practice on it before he comes over."

David continued, "I'm actually going to take them out for dinner while Beth works with you." Glancing up at the clock, he was surprised at how quickly the time had gone by. Jumping up from the chair, he said to Sam, "We better get going. I didn't realize how late it was."

As they both got up David said, "I'm going to run to the restroom. You can go ahead and wait for me in the truck; it's unlocked."

Sam put his bowl and spoon in the kitchen sink, ran a little water in it, and grabbed his book bag. As he neared the front door, he realized that he was about to leave his white envelope that he had placed on the cabinet. Hurrying back to the kitchen, he reached for the envelope beside the refrigerator. With the envelope in his hand, Sam went outside to wait in

David's truck. Shortly thereafter, the two of them were on their way to Beth's apartment. When they arrived, the first thing they saw was Elijah and Molly standing near the door awaiting their dad. Sam could tell they were excited to see their dad and were anticipating having dinner with him. Before leaving, David introduced Sam to them.

"Kids." David said, "This is my friend, Sam Moore."

Both Elijah and Molly looked up at Sam and waved.

"You're really tall." said Molly.

Sam felt shy as a slight smile came to his face.

"Are you going to eat with us?" Molly, ever so curious, asked Sam.

David quickly responded, "Sam is going to stay here and do some fun math work with your Mom."

Molly asked her Dad, "Won't he be hungry? What is he going to eat?"

"Don't worry, We'll bring him something back." David said as he guided the kids out the door. Looking back toward Beth and Sam, he said, "We'll leave you guys to it."

Beth showed Sam to a small table near the kitchen where they took seats across from each other.

"I'm supposed to give this to you." Sam said as he handed the sealed white envelope to Beth.

Beth took the envelope from Sam and opened it. She pulled out the lone sheet of notebook paper that was in it. When she unfolded the paper, Beth saw the words, "Dear Beth" written at the top left corner. When she read the first sentence, an astounded look came to her face. From across the table, Sam watched as her expression changed.

"Are my grades that bad, ma'am?" Sam asked.

Sam had no idea that the envelope he had given her was not the one with his progress report in it. He did not know that he had mistakenly picked up another white envelope from the counter ... the one in which David had put the thoughts he had been recording as a means of self therapy.

Beth's shock was obvious to Sam, but she collected her composure and quenched her urge to keep reading the page-long letter that was filled with a handwriting that she knew was David's. She quickly stuffed the paper back in the envelope and laid it aside.

Beth looked over to Sam and asked, "Grades?"

"Yeah. My teacher put a copy of my progress report from this semester in that envelope."

"Oh, right. No-no they're not ..." Beth said, realizing there must have been a mix up. Whether or not it was intentional, she was unsure; but she immediately had her suspicions.

Beth was noticeably confused as she continued, "Um ... uh, take out any math worksheets you have done in class this week, and we'll start there."

She remained on pins and needles for most of the hour-long session. Her tension grew even more when she heard the sound of her doorbell ringing, followed by several knocks.

Beth, glancing at her watch, said to Sam, "Let's wrap it up for tonight."

While Sam packed up, Beth picked up the envelope and folded it to fit in her pocket. She walked to the door and could hear the children's voices from outside. She opened the door to see them both with half-eaten ice cream cones in their hands.

"Ice cream on a school night?" she asked David, who had a look of guilt on his face.

"I couldn't say no." he replied with a casual laugh.

Beth did her best to play it cool as she wished Sam good luck on the math quiz that he would be taking the next day, and politely told the father of her children to have a good night. She succeeded as David saw nothing out of the ordinary and headed off to take Sam back home. He had absolutely no idea what Beth had in her possession ... no clue that every feeling and thought about Beth, which he had poured out from his soul onto a sheet of notebook paper, was soon to be read by her.

On the way back home, David thought about the notes he had been writing. It had been a few days since he had written anything. He knew, from what Clarence had shared with him about his process, that the next step was to set the envelope aflame. When David arrived home, he went straight to the kitchen for the envelope. He knew it was the perfect night to burn it, so he grabbed a lighter from the kitchen cabinet, stuffed the envelope in his back pocket and headed outside. He opened the sliding glass door that led to the back porch and felt the cool air of an autumn night.

David picked up the small fire pit that had been around for many years and took it a few steps away from the house. He walked back to where he grabbed a handful of leftover firewood thinking that it was being used for a good cause. With the wood in the pit and the sealed white envelope placed on top, David picked up a lawn chair and placed it nearby. Initially he had a tough time getting the fire started, so he added a few of the dry fallen leaves lying in the yard. They did the trick. David took a seat and breathed in the warm smoky air as the flames slowly began charring the wood. His eyes were glued to the envelope when it finally caught fire, and he closely watched as it eventually dissolved into ashes.

David's backyard seemed to have turned into an oasis of serenity as a great sense of peace filled him in the tranquil atmosphere. He sat back and looked up at the smoke that faded into the night sky. In that moment, he knew that he had finally given control to a power that was much higher than his own. That realization made him feel that the heavy burden of emotion that had been weighing on him was lightened. He was totally unaware of the truth of the matter. The words that he thought had gone up in smoke were still on paper, as if written on stone, in the envelope that was now in Beth's possession.

At Clear View High the following morning, Sam Moore strolled into his first period math class full of confidence. Thanks to the tutoring session from the night before, he felt more prepared than ever before. That feeling allowed him to have the strong expectation of immediate positive results. That feeling soon changed when the ten-question quiz was passed out. What he had not realized was that one single hour of review could not make up for the deep hole into which he had dug himself. Before picking up his pencil to begin, Sam held the paper up with both hands and looked at every question on the page. Only two of them were multiple choice. His palms were sweaty, and his legs shook constantly for the hour-long class period. As usual, he was the last one to finish the quiz and did not turn it in until the second period bell sounded. The majority of the time he spent taking the test, Sam could sense that his classmates who had completed the short quiz were irritated. He knew that he was the only reason they had to sit in silence and were unable to enjoy a rare free time.

When everyone stood up to leave the class, the teacher announced, "I will have this graded tonight and will hand them back tomorrow."

That was all Sam could think about for the next twenty-four hours. When the teacher returned the graded quiz the next day, he refused to look at his score while he was in the class. He left the paper folded in his pocket for the rest of the school day, and it stayed there until he got off the bus that afternoon. As he made the short walk from the bus stop to his house, he finally removed the paper from his pocket. For a moment, he just held it in his hand and waited until he reached his front porch steps. Before going up the steps, he slowly unfolded the paper. He sensed a feeling of last minute optimism, but that ended even quicker than it had begun.

At the top of the quiz the grade "55" was circled in red ink. Without examining which answers he had gotten wrong or right, Sam immediately balled up the paper and dropped his head. It took every limited ounce of mental strength he had to remain calm while he walked the few steps up to the front door. He could sense that strength was quickly running out and that familiar feeling of weakness was overtaking him as he entered the house. He tried to push aside his thoughts in fear of what they might lead him to do. He slammed the door closed behind him. Looking straight ahead to the trash can and then to the ball of paper in his right hand, Sam threw the paper across the room. He thought it would go into the trash can, but it was off target and only managed to graze the side of it. He shook his head and walked over to the ball of paper on the floor to pick it up. Before bending down, Sam took a long look at the white plastic trash can. The next thing he knew his right foot was kicking it repeatedly. His kicking eventually knocked over the trash can and everything in it to spilled onto the floor.

"Why did I do that?" he asked himself with regret while looking at the mess he had made. Unable to think of a reasonable answer for his action, he repeated the question to himself … this time much louder. His voice rang out in the empty house as he yelled, "*Why did I do that?!?!*"

Sam bent down on his hands and knees. Grabbing the ball of paper first, he started picking up everything that had fallen out of the trash can. Reflectively, he answered his own question by saying aloud, "Because you don't have any self-control, you angry fool. That's why you did it."

As he stood the trash can back up, he noticed a newspaper among the other things that had fallen out of it. Sam pushed it aside, scooped up the trash and returned it into the trash can. Once all the trash was up, he then picked up the newspaper. As he opened its pages, he noticed a yellow post-it note that had been stuck to a page. It read, "*Joy, thought you'd enjoy this.*" The note had his grandmother's name on it. It was on the front page of the sports section from the local newspaper from the year 1984.

Why would she enjoy this? Sam wondered. He turned the page to see a large black and white picture of a young man wearing the number 13 on a Clear View Vikings jersey. With a basketball in hand, his head was near the rim as he appeared to be going up for a slam dunk. Seeing a reminder of the one thing he loved, basketball, he began to imagine his own picture in a newspaper, and the math grade was quickly forgotten. As he looked deeper into the picture, he saw a great resemblance of himself to the player. Even his braided hair when undone would match the mini afro the young man in the picture was sporting. Wondering if there was any relation, Sam looked for the name of the player in the photo's caption but there appeared to be none. The caption simply read, "*Clear View's Henderson leads the way!*" Sam couldn't think of anyone with that last name.

He turned the page to see another article featuring the state's NFL team that his grandmother was a big fan of. *Maybe this is it?* He guessed while thinking of a reason why someone would have given the old newspaper to her. Remembering he had found it in the trash, he decided that his grandmother couldn't have thought that much of it. Still he was captivated by the picture of the basketball player. He reached into a cabinet drawer, pulled out a pair of scissors, and cut out the picture before tossing the rest of the paper back in the trash. In the grand scheme of things, Sam knew the reason she had it did not really matter. What mattered now was that the intriguing image had fascinated him. The picture of the athlete was not so much about the past, but the future ... his own future. It had appeared at just the right moment to inspire Sam to aim high in a low moment and to strengthen his strive to put on a Clear View basketball jersey himself.

Though there were many areas of his life in which he needed to improve, Sam felt confident that the picture he had just cut from the paper would inspire him to stay the course and continue inching closer to the dream he viewed as his destiny.

Chapter 19

Over one month later

David sat in his living room on a Sunday evening with the sound of a televised NFL game in the background. While Elijah and Molly were occupied in their respective bedrooms, he decided to get a head start on preparing for the varsity basketball tryouts that were to begin the following day. Beth's arrival to pick up the kids came quicker than he had expected. When he heard the doorbell ring, David looked at the clock and was surprised at how quickly the time had passed.

He sat aside his laptop, stood up from the couch and called upstairs, "Kids! Your mom is here. Come on down."

Times together had become quite comfortable between David and Beth in the past months. The arrangement they had agreed upon had led them to a more cordial relationship than they had in years past. David opened the door and welcomed Beth in with a smile as he always did. As they waited for the kids to come down with their bags, their conversation continued. The small talk that had at one time been very tense had actually become quite enjoyable. Even in the recent weeks since Beth had read the deeply personal revelations David had revealed in his letter, she had showed no signs of knowing anything different when she was in his presence. However, every time their paths crossed, Beth made sure she had with her the envelope holding the letter which David thought he had burned on that crisp autumn night.

This routine pick up was no different except for the fact that the contents of the envelope Beth had in her back pocket were starting to eat at her. She had been wanting to return the letter to David for some time. As she stood waiting for the children, she wondered if this should be the time to do it. When the kids came hurrying down the stairs, she was a bit distracted from her thoughts about the letter. However, as they were hugging their father and saying their goodbyes, she knew what she had to do. She walked to the door, opened it, and watched as Elijah and Molly run down the steps and toward the car. She stood to see that they had gotten in the car and the doors were closed. Then she turned back toward David. He saw the wondering look on Beth's face as he told her goodbye; but instead of her usual parting response, she walked back toward him.

"Hey, I almost forgot." Beth said as she reached into her back pocket. "I have something from- I meant *for* you." she said, quickly correcting herself.

She held out the envelope toward him and said, "This is for you."

David took the envelope; and following her to the door, he replied, "Oh, okay. Thanks."

Beth quickly made her way to the car, backed out of the driveway, and sped out of the neighborhood. David wondered what the sudden rush was about as he went back inside to check out the envelope she had given him. He assumed it would be more of the never-ending legal documents from their divorce proceedings. However, when he opened the envelope and saw a single piece of notebook paper folded inside it, he knew that was not the case. He took the paper out, now knowing it was not a legal paper. However, it was not until he read the words *"Dear Beth"* that he looked up from the paper in complete and utter confusion.

What? How? He thought to himself as he pondered how this could be.

"There is no way!" David said when he examined the letter further.

His mind was in turmoil as he attempted to make some sense of it all. He thought back to the day when he had seen the letter burning. He remembered taking it from the cabinet in the kitchen where he left it between his writings. When he thought about the envelope having been on the cabinet, he immediately recalled that Sam had put his envelope containing his progress report on the cabinet too. As he retraced it all time and again in his mind, he could come to no other conclusion except that the two white envelopes had been interchanged.

David thought, *A mix-up. Yes, that's exactly what it was. Sam went to her place for tutoring right after leaving here. That's the only way she could have gotten it.*

Any spark of satisfaction that David might have felt about his quick investigative skills and good memory ended before it could sink in. His thoughts went directly to the almost certain fact that Beth had read the letter. In his dazed state, he folded the paper and opened the envelope to put it back in. That's when he saw a smaller paper with a short note written on it. The note confirmed his thought.

It read, *Your honesty is appreciated. Though I have come to believe that it was never meant for me to read, in the past months I have watched from afar as you have lived out your candid words. It has made all the difference.*

Her nice gesture had little effect on David at that moment. He felt paralyzed with embarrassment. He realized that the letter contained very personal issues of which Beth had no prior knowledge. Despite having been together for over twenty years, he had never mentioned to her any sense of loneliness or regret. Those thoughts were the main theme of the page-long letter. It was partly because David had never truly experienced such deep emotions until the consequences of his years' worth of mistakes came crashing down on him all at once. An even bigger reason was pride in his strong sense of masculinity. That had always hindered him from discussing any subject that he thought might make him seem weak.

After David got over the shock of what had just been revealed to him, he did his best to put the matter aside and get back to work. As a coach, he could not let such thoughts become a distraction at this very important time in his career.

Evaluating any potential talent for his team required total focus. David knew he was lacking it during the two day try-out period. Focus was hard for him to maintain when most of the guys who were trying out seemed to have no focus at all. Sam was the only one who always brought his A-game to the court. He was still working his way toward academic eligibility, so the chances of him playing in the opening game hinged on his upcoming math test. David and Marshal did their best during the tough task of assembling a team that would give them the best chance to be successful.

The first official practice of the year was on Wednesday. That left less than a week to prepare for the first game which was scheduled for Tuesday of the following week. After that practice, Sam would continue his tutoring routine at Beth's apartment. He had developed a great deal of trust in her, especially as he had seen his grades gradually improve. He knew that gave him a much better chance of suiting up in a Clear View jersey.

David took Sam to Beth's apartment and picked up Elijah and Molly for their routine Wednesday dinner and ice cream night. This being the first time he and Beth had seen each other since she had returned the envelope made their encounter more than a little awkward. It seemed that neither of them could find the right words for a meaningful conversation.

As David stood quietly near the door waiting for the children, he realized that he did not know how to recover from this newest roadblock. His mental struggle took him back to Clarence the next afternoon following practice.

"Well, how bad was it?" Clarence asked after he learned that his useful method to work through a tough situation had backfired for David.

David replied, "How bad? I'd say it's pretty bad. It's more humiliating than anything else. She seemed to take it well, but-"

Clarence broke in, "Then it's all good. Son, I promise you'll get over it. Just be glad you didn't say anything bad about her in the letter. If my ex-wife would have seen the first letter I wrote about her, it would've been real rough."

He pulled the sports section out from the local newspaper. "It looks like this is the wrong time of year for you to keep worrying about something like that." Clarence said as he pointed to the High School Basketball Season Preview.

"I haven't even seen that yet." replied David as he took a closer look at the article.

"They've predicted that you'll finish first in the conference again." said Clarence.

"That's all just based on what we did last year and the years before that. They can hardly even name a single player we have on this year's team."

"Yeah, I know you guys lost some talent, but the key to winning nowadays is defense. So many of these teams are so focused on shooting three-pointers and offense. I bet some coaches hardly even coach defense. If your guys can master that, they'll be alright." said Clarence.

"That's a good point. It sounds like I need you on my coaching staff." David replied.

"Well, the game has changed a lot since I played back in the day. Even when my boy played at Clear View, they hardly knew what a three-pointer was. All the action happened under the rim."

David responded in surprise, "After all this time, I didn't know you had all this in you."

"It's all thanks to this right here." Clarence said as he held up the newspaper. "I try to stay well-read on the game. It's how I kept up with it when my son was playing. It pains me to say I never watched him in person."

"Why is that?" asked David.

"I could try and come up with a reasonable answer or excuse, but I don't really have one. I was out and up to no good any time they played, but you can believe I read all about it the next morning. I'd always tell myself that I would go to a game, and I actually made it to the gym entrance one time. But when I saw his mother there inside, I just couldn't bring myself to open the door."

David did not want to go further into Clarence's painful past, so he replied, "You should still come to a game this season. We'd love to have you. I'm sure we're gonna need all the support we can get."

"Well, now that I have an in with the head coach himself, I just might to do that." said Clarence.

Once David left the senior living facility, Clarence kept the basketball season preview article and took it back to his room. He got down on his knees and reached under his bed to pull out the box that had come to be quite heavy. Clarence removed the lid and saw many years' worth of folded written notes. He had been unable to properly dispose of them, so he had just kept cramming them inside. He placed the basketball preview on top of the stack of papers. Lower in the stack were many old sports articles that he had saved from when his estranged son was an athlete at Clear View. Before he placed the lid back on the box, he reached to the bottom of the stack and pulled out several of the articles. For an hour or so, he spent time just sitting there reliving a time when he had failed to make any good memories.

Like Clarence and his collection of old sports articles, Sam Moore also held in his possession a newspaper article that was decades old. It did not matter that the player in the photo was unknown to him. Sam had never really felt it was important to ask his grandmother about it. However, he kept the photo with him at all times. It had become his greatest stress reliever when he found himself in situations of high pressure. Sam's first period math class that Friday morning was exactly that kind of situation. The test he was seconds away from taking would determine whether or not he could suit up and play in the team's first game of the season. What was once a nearly impossible long shot was now only one good grade away. Sam felt his heart pounding as the teacher told everyone to clear off their desks. When she began handing out the test papers, he looked down at the image on the old piece of newspaper that had been folded up to fit in his pocket. It had been folded and unfolded so many time that it was hardly intact. As always, he pictured himself in that same jersey for the game that following Tuesday. He could feel his nerves calming.

"Mr. Moore." the teacher said to get his attention when she walked by his desk with a copy of the test.

Sam took a deep breath as he folded the newspaper image and put it back in his pocket with one hand while receiving his test paper with the other. He knew he would have to wait anxiously all weekend before getting the results back on Monday.

The closer it got to game day, the more his anticipation, as well his confidence in his eligibility, grew. Sam could not stand the idea of leaving school not knowing his score. David also wanted to know if he would have his best player for Tuesday's game before practice began on Monday so he could prepare accordingly. So David made a quick call to his math teacher.

After Sam had dressed into his practice jersey, he sat on a bench in the empty locker room waiting for the practice to start. The other guys were already on the court running around and shooting the ball. Sam was waiting to find out about his math score. He got up and stepped outside in the hallway where David had asked his teacher to meet him. Sam knew by the expression on her face that the news was not good. He had come up just a bit short of the required grade. He fought back tears as he felt his anger trying to kick in, but the newfound perspective that had changed his life kept him from giving in to it. He had finally learned to understand that feeling disappointed and upset was a sign that he cared. He went back into the locker room reflecting on just how far he had come. He knew if he had made it this far, there was no turning back now.

Sam left the locker room and walked up to Coach Jackson to give him the news for which he had been waiting.

"So?" David, feeling hopeful, asked Sam when he saw him approaching.

"Nah, but I came close." Sam replied.

"Oh, man. It's all good. Are you okay?" asked David.

"Yes, sir. As long as I can still practice."

"Of course, you need to lock these guys up on defense to give them an idea of what they'll have coming tomorrow." David said with a laugh.

As Sam turned around and continued walking onto the court, David said, "Hey, Sam." When Sam turned around David told him, "I'm really proud of you."

Once practice came to an end, David gave Sam a ride home as he always did. To their surprise they saw a car in the driveway which was usually empty when David dropped him off.

"You have company." said David.

"That's Grandma's car." Sam replied, knowing it was a rare thing for her to be home that early in the evening.

Sam went inside to find his grandmother preparing dinner. She had a bright smile on her face.

"There's my boy." she said.

"How did you beat me home today?" asked Sam.

"I was able to leave early today. Another nurse accidentally showed up to watch Mrs. Johnson, but I let her take over so I could take off."

"Great." Sam said while taking in the aroma of dinner on the stove.

"Your teacher called me today." his grandmother said.

"Yeah?" asked Sam.

"She said you're almost eligible and she's offered to give you a chance for extra credit so you can play in the big game on Friday."

"Really? Really?" Sam said. When she nodded her head yes, Sam expressed his joy by jumping up and touching the ceiling with his hand. "Wow! I can't believe it! That's good to hear. The Western View game is a big one, they're our rivals."

"Yeah. She said something about a picture of a basketball player that you always have on you that must be your good luck charm."

"Oh, yeah I guess it helps." Sam said.

As his grandmother continued to tend to dinner on the stove, she asked, "What is it, just one of your favorite NBA players or something?"

"Actually," Sam said as he dug in his book bag to retrieve the image, "I don't know who it is. Some random guy from a long time ago at Clear View. All I know is that his last name is Henderson."

His grandmother stopped what she was doing and asked, "His last name is what?"

"Henderson." Sam replied.

His grandmother knew that name, which was once her own, all too well. When she turned around to see Sam holding the picture for her to look at, the young man in it was definitely no random guy.

Thinking that the article and image had been discarded, she asked Sam, "Where did you-Uh … How did you get that?"

"I actually found it in the trash." Sam said as he began to realize that the image likely held some significance for his grandmother. He felt inclined to ask, "Who is it?" Sam went closer to her and held up the image so she could see it more clearly. He continued, "Who is this in the picture?"

His grandmother said nothing as she backed up and put one hand onto the counter while placing the other one over her mouth. Her reaction only increased Sam's desire for an answer. His tone became more desperate, "Just say something ... anything!"

"Sam." she said, "That is my son ... your uncle."

Sam looked back at the image in the ragged piece of newspaper in his hand. Now he could see it in a totally new light. His mind went back to the day he had found it. The small note that had been attached to the newspaper made sense now, as did the reason why someone would have given it to his grandmother. However, in Sam's mind, something still did not add up; so his first question was not about the uncle, whose existence he never knew about, but was one that his grandmother had not expected to ever have to answer.

"Then why did I find it in the trash?" he asked her.

"Oh, Sam!" his grandmother replied while approaching him and placing her hand on his shoulder. "There's just too much pain, I could not stand to hold onto it."

"What happened?" Sam asked.

"Your Uncle Jesse fell off the deep end not long after this photo was taken. Boy, he was a star. That court was the one place he had control of himself; but the moment he stepped off of it, all hell broke loose. His invincible mindset killed him. It hurts so much to know that I, along with everyone else in his life, enabled him to get away with anything."

Even though Sam could picture himself in the newspaper image, he knew very well that he was much like the Jesse she was describing. To change the topic, he asked, "So where'd the name 'Henderson' come from?" knowing that he and his grandmother both had the same last name.

"That was my husband's last name. Once he was gone and out of the picture, and after Jesse passed on, I wanted my young daughter and I to break away from that past. 'Moore' was my maiden name and has been my last name since then.

"I guess it didn't have too much of an effect on Mama." Sam said, knowing she had been behind bars for most of his life.

"Sam." his grandmother said, "Look at me. Look in my eyes."

He slowly lifted his head and looked at her while she said, "There's nothing you or I can do about what has already happened. It does you no good to even try. I've spent so much time with regret that I missed out on what was happening right in front of me. Don't make the same mistake."

Sam nodded, but he knew that escaping the past was not an easy thing to do, especially after learning so much about it. The next day he found himself sitting on the team bench in the opposing school's gym while watching his teammates warm up for their first game of the season. Dressed nicely in business casual attire, Sam represented Clear View well; but he would have given anything to be in basketball shorts and shoes. While longing to have a basketball in hand, Sam thought about the image of his uncle. Knowing who it was in the picture gave the newspaper cutout even more meaning for him.

"You okay?" David asked Sam after taking a seat beside him on the bench.

"Yeah, I'm good." Sam replied to the question that his coach frequently asked him.

"What do you have there?" asked David when he saw the old piece of newspaper.

"Oh, this is my uncle, Jesse Henderson."

"*Jesse Henderson.*" David said aloud, "I think I remember that name. He was several years ahead of me. I see he's wearing the number that you chose."

"Yeah, number thirteen. I'm ready to wear it myself." said Sam.

"I know you are, Buddy. It'll only be a matter of time before a picture is taken of you wearing that Clear View jersey."

"I feel like I've already seen it a thousand times in my head." Sam replied.

"I've seen it too, and soon everybody else will." David said. He continued, "Look, I know it sucks having to sit here feeling helpless today, but try to cheer the guys on tonight. They're gonna need it."

There was no amount of cheering that the team could have received to give them any chance at victory. What softened the blow of a twenty-point loss for David was the fact that he had spent all off season bracing for such a result. The score of the defending champion's first game was much more of a shock to the spectators who were on the outside looking in.

David arrived home the next evening after a long day that had included putting his team through a brutal session of practice, driving Sam to and from tutoring, then having dinner with his kids. There had been no time to check his phone since the first game. After finally getting to sit down, David scanned through loads of unread messages, missed calls, and unanswered emails. Most of the attempts to reach him had come in late on the previous evening from local sports journalists wanting him to comment on his team's defeat.

David had no desire to spend his night reading up on articles written about his team or responding to any messages sent to him. He tossed his phone aside and went to the kitchen to make a bowl of cereal. He noticed the rarely used house phone's answering machine light was blinking. David walked over and pressed the play button. As it activated, he heard Clarence's raspy voice in his distinctive pace of talking.

"I hope this finds you well, David. I got this number from the phonebook. I also read about the game, but I know your guys will bounce back. Come by and visit before too long, I have something here to show you … it's worth seeing."

When David squeezed in time to go to the senior living facility the next day, he hoped what Clarence had to show him was not related to the opening game. Even before the final buzzer sounded, he had tried to move on from it. He was now completely focused on the big rivalry game against Western View High. When Clarence appeared in the sitting room holding several newspapers in his hand, David wondered if the visit was a mistake.

"What do you have there?" David nervously asked.

Clarence said nothing while carefully sitting down and moving his cane out of the way.

"I thought you'd maybe like to see these." Clarence replied while placing the papers on the coffee table.

David could then see that the newspaper articles were older and asked, "Oh, are these from back when I was playing?" thinking Clarence had possibly spotted a picture of him.

Clarence thought back to the years his son was in high school and realized that David was several years younger. He replied, "Actually, these are a little before your time there."

He unfolded one paper and while looking for the article, Clarence told David, "These all feature my boy that I mentioned the other day."

"Oh, that's right." said David. "This is how you kept up with him playing, right?"

"That's true, yes; but it's become more than that. This, to me, is treasure. It's what keeps his memory alive. See, my boy is gone. I had originally saved them to remember his playing days, but they've become memories of a short life that I didn't have much part of."

Clarence finally found the article he was looking for and pointed to the image that featured his son and another Clear View player in action. One of the players wore a Clear View jersey with the number thirteen on it. The other player was wearing number eleven. David's first observation when he saw the picture was that the player was wearing number thirteen. His thoughts immediately went to Sam. *That's Sam's number.* Then, *Sam chose that number because of his uncle.* Lastly, *is that Sam's uncle? No! It can't be. There's no way.*

In hopes of clarifying, David asked, "Uh, so- Which one is your son?"

"Right here where my finger is pointing, number thirteen." said Clarence.

David tried to think of the image that Sam had shown him, but he could not remember enough detail to determine whether or not it was the same player wearing number thirteen.

"And his name?" asked David.

"I think it shows it right here." Clarence said while turning the paper around, looking closely at the photo's caption and then further down in the article. "Oh here it is … Jesse Henderson."

Jesse Henderson? I've heard that before. Then David remembered that he had heard the name from Sam who had, just a few days earlier, identified him as his uncle. David's inner voice screamed, *Jesse Henderson!*

"Je-Jesse Henderson, your son?" asked David.

Clarence nodded before hearing David reword the same question, "You are telling me that Jesse Henderson is YOUR son!!"

"Have you heard of him?" Clarence asked.

David was in deep thought as he compared what he had heard to a complicated word problem, *"If Jesse Henderson is Sam's uncle and also Clarence's son then …"*

As he tried to reason out the possible relation between the two people that he had spent more time with in recent months than anyone else, David replied, "I-I think I have heard of him. Yeah."

"That comes as a surprise. Most people have probably tried to do everything they can to forget about my boy." Clarence said.

David, whose thoughts were all over the place as he replied, "I think that-uh, I think that I know someone who wouldn't mind knowing more about your son, and maybe about you as well."

"I find that hard to believe." said Clarence.

"Trust me." David said, "I understand. I'm also finding things hard to believe right this minute."

David suddenly realized that he really didn't need to say any more. It would be better for Clarence to have the opportunity to make the connection himself.

"Clarence, all I can say is that you should really find a way to get to tomorrow's game." David said while standing up from his chair, knowing he had to continue preparing for it.

"Well, okay then. Whatever you say, Coach." Clarence replied.

"It starts at seven o'clock. Does someone need to pick you up?"

"No." Clarence said, "I'll find a way."

Chapter 20

The stage was set for cross-town rivals to face off on a Friday evening in the Clear View High School gymnasium. The teams were evenly matched and though they were both in rebuilding seasons, it was guaranteed not to have much impact on the quality of the intense match up. Every year, despite each team's record or talent on the roster, the games always came down to the wire and had resulted in many memorable finishes. This caused nearly the entire area to shut down as everyone flocked to the school to take in the action.

The gym began to fill up quickly as the girls' varsity game came to an end. Coach David Jackson peaked his head out from the locker room hall door to see the expiring time on the scoreboard. He walked back into the boys' locker room where his players were anxiously waiting to take the court. David walked to the center of the room and stood in front of the team.

"Okay, fellas." He said, "Clean slate … we have a clean slate."

This reigned true, especially for Sam Moore, who, thanks to the extra credit assignment, was about to play in his first ever high school game.

"Hey, you guys know what to do." David assured them. However, that did not calm Sam's nerves since his focus was on the noise of the crowd in front of which he was about to play. David's loud voice echoed in the locker room as he finished his pep talk to the team.

By the time both teams took the court for warm ups, the bleachers were almost completely filled. People were still standing in line just outside the gym doors waiting to get in. They didn't know just what a good show was in store as the game proved to live up to the unending hype that surrounded the rivalry. From the start, Sam was very grateful for the many afternoons he had spent conditioning on the same court. It prepared him for what would be a very physical game between the two teams with both of them giving every ounce of effort they had.

For those watching, it was hard to take their eyes off of the intense action between the players on the court; but David found himself doing just that. He constantly eyed over to the gym doors hoping to see Clarence make his way in. Though the harsh past and limited mobility of his newfound friend and confidant made the invitation to attend the game a stretch, it was very important to David for him to be there. The connection he had discovered between Clarence and Sam the day before was still hard for him to comprehend. To think that Clarence's son was very possibly the father of one of his favorite teens was not a minor issue in David's mind. Even so, regardless of what he had learned and if it really was true, David knew it was not his place to tell it. He had thought long and hard about it and had come to the conclusion that, if their paths were meant to cross, it should happen naturally without his assistance.

Shortly after the second quarter began, David's focus was on the game when Sam was fouled hard in mid-air after driving strongly to the basket. When he landed hard onto the court, the entire gym let out a shared gasp. Silence followed as Sam laid flat on his back surrounded by his teammates. Just as David and the other coaches were approaching him, Sam slowly stood to his feet.

A timeout was called before the free-throws would be shot. As Sam entered the huddle David asked him the expected question, "You okay?"

Sam gave his usual response, "Yeah, I'm good." Then, with a smile, he responded, "I just needed to catch my breath." as he gulped down a bottle of water.

David's head was entirely in the game after setting their defense and sending the players back on the court. All eyes were on Sam, who stood at the free-throw line to attempt two shots. Nobody, not even David, noticed the gym door open when an older gentleman with a cane and a man beside him dressed in scrubs came in. Clarence had indeed found a way to show up with the help of one of the senior living workers. Though the Western View supporters grew loud in hopes of distracting Sam's free-throw shooting, the intense environment felt nearly silent to Clarence. His lack of hearing was in no way a reason for it though. The young man getting ready to shoot was the first person Clarence saw in the packed gym. He was standing at the free throw line with the ball in his hands and the number thirteen on his jersey. Clarence blinked a few times at the sight of the player shooting the first free throw which was off target.

The facility worker guided him in further and they both stood with their backs against the wall. As Sam got himself together before attempting the second free-throw, he gazed straight ahead and then slightly to his right. For a brief moment, he locked eyes with an older gentleman without having any idea of the strong effect it had on the old man. The eye contact couldn't have lasted for more than a blink at most; but in that half second, Clarence saw the spitting image of his children. The eyes that had met his resembled his daughter's eyes, and the similar facial features of the young man at the basket and his son were undeniable. In that short moment, Clarence saw before him the culmination of everything he had left behind. Then and there, Clarence needed nothing more to assure him that the young man was a blood relative.

Clarence eventually found a seat on the first row of bleachers next to the wall on his right with everyone else in the bleachers to his left and above him. The worker who had driven him there remained standing by the gym doors while Clarence continued to take in his first live sporting event in years. During the half time break, his eyes searched around the gym looking for any familiar faces in the crowd. He had been out of circulation so long that there were very few people he recognized. He enjoyed the atmosphere even though his mind was still on the strong likeness of the boy shooting free throws and his own children.

Just then the buzzer sounded for the start of the second half of the game. Almost simultaneously, Sam's grandmother, Joy Moore, quietly made her way into the gym. After a long day at work, she had finally arrived. She made every effort to get there to watch Sam play. Prior to tonight, Sam had been unable to contain his behavior and remain on a team long enough to play in many games.

She walked directly in front of Clarence, but with his back to the wall and his eyes intently on the court, he didn't notice her. However, from the corner of his eye, he had recognized her as she joined several other women who had made room for her to sit a couple of rows up. Clarence immediately lowered his head and slouched down in hopes that Joy would not notice his presence at the game.

"Mr. Henderson" the facility worker said as he approached Clarence, "Is something wrong. Why are you sitting like that? You know it isn't good for your back."

"It'll have to be for a little while." Clarence replied as he crunched a little lower.

Seeing Joy at the game confirmed his suspicion that there was a strong resemblance of his own children in the player wearing number thirteen. He immediately knew that the likelihood of that young man coming from one of his own children was high. That being the case, Clarence wondered more. Would the boy have inherited the bad traits of his children? If so, why would his grandmother even come to the game? Was his playing in this game a one-time event? Would the boy lose his temper any minute now? Wretched thoughts filled Clarence's mind. Those thoughts periodically recurred throughout the entire second half of the game, but he did not let them completely distract him.

Clarence simply could not keep his eyes off of number thirteen. It was not only his looks that pointed toward a Henderson descent; it was also the way he took over the action-packed game. There was no more than a two possession separation between the two rivals as they went back and forth in the final stretch of the game. With less than a minute left to go, Western View managed to secure a three-point lead. David Jackson called a timeout to set up a play on offense in response to their last basket. When the game continued, a Clear View player made an inbound pass to the point guard who quickly passed the ball to their freshman star player.

Everyone on the Clear View team seemed to step aside as Sam Moore had the ball in his hands with only seconds remaining. He dribbled to his right but got jammed up and had to pass the ball to a nearby teammate. Sam quickly made himself open and got the ball back with only ten seconds remaining. Needing a three-pointer to tie the game, Sam backed up behind the arc and quickly glanced up at the clock. The crowd noise echoed loudly as many screamed, "Shoot it!!" Sam stepped back and created enough separation to get a good shot off. After the ball was in the air, he, along with everyone else, could feel that it was going in. The ball, that seemed to be on target, moved in what felt like slow motion to everyone watching. Just after the buzzer sounded, the ball bounced off the rim, proving it was too strong of a shot.

The game was over and the Western View players and supporters celebrated their hard fought victory as the home crowd and team stood silently, feeling the disappointment of defeat. Sam was visibly crushed. He remained in place on the same spot he had just misfired the game-tying shot. His teammates kept their distance from him. They were afraid of what might result if they overstepped their bounds with Sam. There was only one person who could approach Sam at that moment. After shaking hands with the opposing coaching staff, David Jackson jogged over to Sam and guided him toward the sideline.

With his arm around Sam's shoulder, David said, "Man, I'm so proud of you!"

As they walked off the court, Sam lifted his head. He looked straight at David and said, "I missed it, Coach. I really missed the shot."

"Yeah, you did this time." replied David, "But think of how many more you're going to make. This is just the start of something great."

"You think so?" asked Sam who was fighting back tears.

David smiled and replied, "I've seen it in my head a thousand times."

When the gym began to clear out, the facility worker thought it was best for Clarence to avoid exiting along with the crowd of people jamming the doors. While they remained seated, Clarence looked over his shoulder to see that Joy was still seated in the bleachers chatting with a few other ladies in the group with which she sat for the game. After a few minutes went by, he saw those other people walk past him as they left the gym. Clarence felt that the unimaginable was happening when he looked in Joy's direction again to see her seated alone in the same spot she had occupied during the game.

The facility worker took a look at the gym's exit doors. The way out was nearly cleared "Okay, Mr. Henderson, we can head out now." he said.

Clarence grabbed his cane from the floor and stood up to follow the worker out of the gym. He took one step toward the exit and then stopped.

"Wait right here." Clarence told the worker, "I'll be right back."

While he slowly walked in Joy's direction, Clarence could not believe what he was doing. He felt as if he had lost control of his own body. He felt the same lack of control when he found himself speaking to Joy.

"Hello, Mrs. Henderson?" said Clarence.

Joy's back was in his direction as she was standing to collect her purse and sweater. When she heard the voice, she continued collecting her items.

Before turning around, she said, "Now, sir. You're terribly mistaken, I haven't been Mrs. Henderson for a long time. Did you know me way back then?" Do you want to explain yourself?"

Joy, not hearing any response, turned around to see Clarence Henderson meekly standing before her.

Taken aback, she cleared her throat. "Ahem ... D-do you want to explain yourself?" she said in an obviously confused tone of voice.

Clarence did not even attempt to say anything as his lips began to quiver. He could feel the tears building up in his eyes. One blink later, they were flowing down his cheeks as everything within seemed to come unleashed. There was no controlling his emotions, so Clarence put his hand over his face and wept bitterly.

Joy could not believe her eyes. What she was seeing explained so much to Joy. As she gazed at Clarence in his broken state, she became emotional herself. She had no idea what to say or do next. She had become so lost in the emotional state of her helpless ex-husband that she did not realize her grandson was watching everything unfold from a distance.

Joy heard footsteps from behind her and turned to see Sam walking in her direction. He was carrying his gym bag and had a puzzled look on his face. Joy could tell by his expression on Sam's face that he would have many questions to ask when he got home. They would be concerning what he had just seen, and she would have no choice but to truthfully answer them.

Back in the coach's office, after Assistant Coach Lee had left, David Jackson took a seat in the chair at his desk. He leaned back and propped his feet on the edge of the desk. He was trying to relax, but his mind was recapping the game his team had just barely lost. He intended to soon head out for the usual routine of his weekends without his kids. He would begin with a take-out meal and after that watch film. Just as he was about to get up and leave, his cell phone buzzed. He picked it up from his desk to see a text notification from Beth.

"There are some people waiting to see you by the hallway trophy case."

Assuming that it was Beth with the children, David couldn't imagine why they would be waiting there. He knew them well enough to know that any sporting event was the last place they would want to be.

Hurriedly grabbing his bag and locking up the office, David walked down the hall and made his way to the trophy case. When he turned the corner, he could see them ahead in the distance down the long hallway. David walked toward Beth and the kids without saying anything while Beth looked down at her phone. The kids were looking at all the shiny trophies behind the glass case. Just before he reached them, Molly happened to look up and see her father approaching.

"There he is!" she said.

David could not help but smile. With his arms held out he asked, "What are you guys doing here?"

"The kids insisted on coming." Beth said.

"Really? They did?" asked David.

"Well, it turns out that they don't get bored when we show up with only a few minutes remaining in the game."

"Good solution." David said with a laugh.

"Dad, Sam would have made that last shot if he had watched my guys play on the basketball video game." Elijah said.

David replied, "Oh yeah? That's a thought! And at this point, I'll try any method of coaching."

"Kids, go over and wait for us by the doorway." Beth said, pointing ahead.

David would have much rather had the kids stay around to help keep his nerves in tow. As he watched the children walk away, his mind went back to a time many years ago when he and Beth had stood in that same place together. That was where their relationship had begun. Then he instantly remembered that the two of them had barely been able to make conversation since the letter debacle. Beth noticed his uneasy feeling and wanted desperately to address it.

She ended the uncomfortable silence by saying, "On our way here, the kids suggested that I join them at the weekly ice cream spot where you take them."

"Oh. Yeah, you definitely should." David responded in a somewhat surprised tone. "They'll probably be up all night; but, hey, it's Friday."

"If you don't mind, I will. I think they'd love that. It would be good for them." She replied.

"Good for them or you as a mother wanting the kids to see their parents act normally?" David responded.

Trying to keep her voice down, she said, "David, I'm not- I just cannot do this back and forth with you anymore. I don't want to."

"I don't either. I'm sorry." said David.

"No. Don't worry about it." she responded.

"Really, I am sorry." said David. "For the letter especially. That just messed things up even more between us, and it wasn't necessary. It was a big mix up and-"

Beth broke in to put an end to his explanation and said, "Stop it, David. Just stop."

David backed down and became quiet as Beth continued, "I can now see a glow in my ... *our* children's eyes when they talk about their father. That's what matters for now, forget about anything else."

As she spoke, Beth felt a similar aura coming from him as she looked deeply in his eyes. She no longer saw him as the man who had been blinded by his own egocentric mindset.

"Okay." David responded, "Yes, you're absolutely right."

"If we want what's best for them," she said, pointing to the kids ahead, "we have to be a team. It's all about them."

As David nodded, Beth continued to look directly in his eyes.

"Who are you?" she asked him, seeing no sign of a coach who had just lost a tough game.

With no hesitation, David replied, "I'm Elijah and Molly's father, a teammate of Beth, and a man who is about to have ice cream for dinner."

Beth was filled with relief when she saw David's smile break through.

"Let's have at it." she said. They met Molly and Elijah at the door, and the four of them walked out of the school as a family.

They quickly learned that not living together under the same roof did not mean that they were broken. Realizing that, their relationship grew to be much closer than it had ever been before. The bond they soon established was one that would not require David and Beth to be in love. All they needed to do was show love, and that is what they learned to do. Their love was evident during every future holiday, birthday, and school function. Saved seats were no longer left empty. Phone calls were always promptly returned. A busy schedule was no longer an excuse to avoid responsibility. By giving love as a parent, David enjoyed the rewards of the presence of his children and watching them grow up. He now took advantage of every opportunity to be with them. Love could be felt in something as simple as seeing their smiles. For David, love was seen in something as big as hearing his son give his first vocal performance in an auditorium packed full of people. He now knew that life was so much better when love prevailed.

That healing love was not only confined to David's family. It contagiously spread like a wildfire to their friends who so needed it. Three years later, on Sam Moore's senior night, David took great pride in seeing him locked arm-in-arm with Grandma Joy to his right and the man Sam had come to know as "Papa Henderson" to his left. As they escorted him onto the court before his final game at Clear View High, a new banner was unveiled in his honor. Sam Moore had become the first player in the history of Clear View High School to score 2,000 career points. This accomplishment helped earn him a full-ride college basketball scholarship. In his four-year high school basketball career, he had rarely ever missed a practice, never missed a single game, and was never intimidated on the court.

Because Coach David had given him guidance and helped him find direction ...

Because a teacher named Beth had tutored him to help him with his academics ...

Because he had realized that his Grandmother Joy cared about his future ...

Because Clarence Henderson had taken pride in his grandson ...

Because of love ...

Sam had beat all the odds ...

Epilogue

Love in its truest form came to Clarence in his final years. He lived his last days in joy and peace in the home from which he had been so absent in his younger years. He was cared for by the woman he had once avoided at all costs. As they got to know each other again, he learned to appreciate her in a way that he never had in their youth. They enjoyed their togetherness until his end ... and then the new life Clarence had decided to live was greatly celebrated.

What lived on were the lessons that had changed his life. Those lessons, which he had generously shared, eventually helped many others along the way. It all began when a man sought him out ... a man who was on a desperate search for answers. By seeing life from another man's perspective, Coach David Jackson found answers to his own issues, proving that the way to redemption cannot be traveled alone.

Made in the USA
Monee, IL
09 September 2021